THE LONG RETURN
HOME

FLAVIO GIRARDELLI

Youcanprint *Self-Publishing*

Title | The Long Return Home
Author | Flavio Girardelli
ISBN | 978-88-91165-98-5
Translation by Mary Purpari
Cover by Uniquedesignxx www.melarts.com
Photo by Flavio Girardelli - Cima d'Asta e Caldenave

Youcanprint Self-Publishing
Via Roma, 73 - 73039 Tricase (LE) - Italy
www.youcanprint.it
info@youcanprint.it
Facebook: facebook.com/youcanprint.it
Twitter: twitter.com/youcanprintit

SUMMER

Summer. Sunday, the sun is high and warm; the horizon seems to float, almost dancing thanks to the humidity rising from the asphalt. A group of friends heading towards Garda Lake in a van, the Volkswagen Kombi that they affectionately called Chamomile, because of its performance on the road. It was a slightly faded sky-blue, with several designs on its sides: an enormous guitar on the left and a huge eagle on the right. It carried a long clump of wire on the bumper, a subterfuge found after an incautious reverse where Lorenzo discovered for himself that even low walls are not easily bent. They hoped they wouldn't be stopped by the police, who would have had a very good excuse to slap them with a very heavy fine or even sequester the vehicle. Poor thing, this van was very old, as could be seen even from inside: the red cloth seats, now completely thread-bare, barely acknowledging their original color, although all kinds of stains were very much visible, and the dashboard was completely covered with stickers and various graffiti. Peter, Giorgio's German uncle who lived in Hannover, had given it to him for his eighteenth birthday; he had taken care of it for many years for the nephew who, just like him, played in a band and in whom he saw himself as a young man. His friends defined Chamomile as "the legend" because they had faced so many battles together with her ever since they were eighteen year olds: concerts, the mountains, the sea, adventures through half of Italy and even excursions abroad.

Their feet were hanging down out of the window, while singing songs by Vasco, Ligabue, Springsteen, Bob Marley, ending up by shouting out a couple by groups in the area – for example the famous Bastard; the frenetic music of the Squirties – the band in which their good friend Joe Barbarossa (the nickname given to him because of his long red beard and Rasta-style dreads) played. There was a festive, holiday feeling in the air after months of hard work; a somewhat heavy air, at least inside the van, since they had celebrated practically until dawn and all sorts of odors floated inside there. The seats were full of crumbs and a few beer cans rolled aimlessly on the floor. A black sock also flew dangerously around, swishing its foul odor here and there, but no one accepted the responsibility of recognizing it as theirs. They were childhood friends, all of them around twenty-three years old. They had left their girlfriends at home for a get-together among friends, just like in the old days. A weekend together after three long years was just what the doctor had ordered. They had become children again during the get-together; a day at the lake, and they were lost, just like in the old days. Only Alessandro was missing from the group, because his girlfriend just hadn't wanted him to go with them. She said that they led him astray. She was so delusional... the poor thing thought she had put him on the straight and narrow by taking him to church and never letting him go out in the evening unless it was with her. Sure, she kept him in line, but the segregator didn't know that, whenever it was possible, her dear Alessandro also went out happily with her best friend. Even better – always behind her back – he escaped with his co-workers to drink a few beers and, every once in a while, a toccata and fugue at night to enjoy a few strippers. Anyway, now they were traveling and who wasn't there, well, that was too bad, because he was certainly missing a good time with his friends.

And among those friends were Giorgio the hippie and Giorgio the head-banger, who played the electric guitar for a group in the area. He had a big tattoo shaped like an eagle on his back, while a Gibson towered proudly on his breast, right where his heartbeat. And that's not even counting the eight earrings spread out on his earlobes or the piercings – one on his right nipple and the other on his nose. He had music in his blood and many appreciated it, not just the metal fans, but even the girls went crazy for this damned man. But he was a serious and faithful boy; he had already been together with his Patty, who followed him enthusiastically to all of his concerts, for five years. He never even considered cheating on her, nor to even doubt their story; they were a beautiful couple and were both deeply in love. All of them, good or bad, had tried to play something as teenagers, first the guitar and then something else. They were often overcome by their enthusiasm and the sense of emulating their idols, but they were easily discouraged right after their first attempts and mediocre results. Among the group of friends, he was the only one who ended up continuing to cultivate this passion; unfortunately, even though he was good, the music wasn't enough to live on. But the satisfaction was so great that Giorgio hadn't given up and alternated his evenings between concerts and working as a bartender in a small bar along the main road of the Valsugana.

Then, there was Shy Lorenzo, certainly the quietest among them, with his head screwed on straight: even if the world should fall apart, he wouldn't. He had gotten his friends out of trouble more than once, intervening at the first sign of a fight or taking them home when they were pitifully drunk. He was about six feet tall and weighed about two-hundred pounds, with a round, peaceful face, black hair, green eyes and a pleasant smile. His nose was very pronounced and because of this was nick-named "the big eagle". He couldn't conceive betrayal or superficiality. He was finishing up his studies as a mechanical engineer and was doing very well; he saw his future probably opening up in one of the area's companies, where there was never a lack of work in that sector.

Another member of the company, who undoubtedly never went unnoticed, was Augusto, known as "the colossus": gigantic, six feet six inches tall and two-hundred sixty-four pounds. To his mother, he was a doctor lost, because she would have liked to see him in a white jacket whereas he had chosen to become an architect. He still had a few more exams to take and his doctoral thesis to write, but he already knew that he had a brilliant life and a future rich with great opportunities ahead of him. Several technical studios had come forward, offering him a post-graduate apprenticeship, but anyway, as the son of a well-known, rich builder of dams and bridges who did a lot of work in China, Augusto knew that the near future would take him there. His passion for food equaled that for the women that he continuously tried to win over thanks to his great innate pleasantness. In case of need, he used his wallet, never sadly empty, and his physical attraction: despite his stature, his face was well-featured and gave a sensation of delicate sweetness. In addition, he knew how to behave in a kind and friendly manner. In short, he was a ladies' man. Once he had won his prey over, sooner or later he ended up by cheating on her. He just couldn't stay faithful!

6

And then there was Emanuele, defined the teetotaler by his friends, who was presently at the van's wheel. Actually, he had had a couple of glasses, but just wine, and only what he himself had produced. Unlike the others, he was born outside the province of Trento, in the zone surrounding Verona. He moved to the Trentino county seat with his family when he was a child, because of his father's work as an important company leader. At first, the move had traumatized him, but then he settled down. When he finished middle school and then trade school, he began to pursue a great passion born in the splendid countryside surrounding Verona, a passion that soon became his business: a vintner, and in just a few years he had also opened a small wine-cellar where he proudly sold his unbottled wine. Emanuele was the only one in the group that had already set the basis for a solid future for his family, in which he obviously contemplated marriage with his adored Giuliana.

They arrived at the parking lot along the lake. It was strange, but the sunny day hadn't given rise to the crowd that usually invaded the parking lots and paths around the lake in a chaotic manner. Having parked Chamomile, they headed off – backpacks in place – towards a strip of beach where they had often spent their weekend since they were eighteen. That beach was truly beautiful, near a park, with a stand for getting something to drink or eating an ice cream. There was a small dock a few yards further on: you could listen to the breaking of the waves which then formed clouds of drops that were carried away by the breeze. The low turnout allowed them to pick their places and to delimit the best area with their towels. The spectacular reflection of the light on the lake caused the water and the entire area surrounding it to shimmer. They put on their bathing suits and rubbed a minimal amount of sun screen on their skin, convinced that otherwise they wouldn't get even a hint of color, except for Lorenzo who was more worried about getting a sunburn than a great tan. He used almost half a tube of maximum strength sun screen, enough cream to completely smear face and body with an oily, white coating. His friends never missed the chance to make fun of him when he did this. Lorenzo had an obsessive terror of getting sunburnt because once, at the beach, when he was very young, his mother had settled him down on a lounge chair, with half of his body in the shade and his legs exposed to the sun's rays; at the end of the day they found him practically burned.

They stretched out on the towels and began to enjoy a little sun on their skin. Other people arrived during the next few hours to savor the spectacular day, just like them. Couples, singles, groups of friends, characters with absurd bathing suits that obviously gave them a reason for joking and laughter. Then, when the girls walked by, they went vague and pretended to look in another direction, but they sized them up from the corner of their eyes, pausing to look at the parts they considered the most interesting. That is, until a girl in a topless bathing suit walked by. At that point, Augusto started to stand up and head towards her, but they grabbed him by a leg, pulled him back down to the ground and jokingly attacked him – while everyone laughed on – with newspapers, towels and whatever else they happened to find at the moment.

It was seven o'clock a.m., but Francesca couldn't wait to leave her hotel room to spend the last day of her vacation in Trentino. She was in seventh heaven after having recently obtained her doctorate in economy and business. Once the summer was over she would begin her professional apprenticeship with an important job with a company in Vicenza, but above all, she would be going to live on her own, far from home and without her parents following her. When she received her degree, they had given her a vacation and they had a second gift ready for her upon her return, the fruit of a promise made to her when she began her studies at the university: a ticket for a trip to Japan.

Her parents had a big company of aerospace products in Padua. Her father was from the area, but her mother was originally from Calabria. They met during a vacation where Raimondo, Francesca's father, went to Tropea. He noticed her immediately, that splendid, dark-skinned girl: the big, deep black eyes, large breasts and wide hips. The classic Mediterranean girl. With a little work, he had been able to wrangle a date with her, with others following after. In fact, they had dated during the entire vacation period, going out together in the afternoons or evenings. She worked in the country, and as soon as possible she would search for any excuse to leave her parents and go meet Raimondo. The day before he left, enveloped by the fragrance of saltiness and passion and the intimacy of a starless night, they made love in the sand designed by their bodies, on a small beach, hidden among the reefs. Raimondo was contacted a couple of months after returning home by her parents, furious because their daughter was expecting. Following the customary explanations from both sides, the relationship between them, at first very tense and complicated, was soon resolved and became very friendly; however, the two lovers' embarrassment was alive, they were scrutinized with good-natured severity by everyone as they just stood there, looking into each other's eyes, hand in hand, without saying a word. In the end, everyone agreed that the young couple would get married, despite the young age and the brief engagement, to "repair" what had happened. Maria and Raimondo conceived Francesca on that warm, accommodating beach, on that night full of their love. Now, they were about forty-five years old, and after more than twenty years their life as a couple was still intense, always in love and always together.

Francesca was very much fascinated by the country of the Rising Sun. She liked everything about Japan: from the tiny bonsai – she had four at home – and the harmony between past and present, traditional and modern, to the gigantic populated metropolis and their apparent chaos, where respect for rules, people and an almost maniacal organization reigned. She was madly in love with sushi and that delicately refined way of preparing all food. She loved the oriental culture, the civilization and traditions of the empire, the Samurai and the geishas. She even loved the manga comics, and considered the Japanese eroticism excellent and intriguing. Like her mother, she was splendidly dark, five feet, three inches tall, deep black eyes, very light skin that immediately took on an olive tinge in the sun, taking on amber-toned lights. Her shoulder-length hair was done up in braids; she looked like a Medusa—don't look her in the eyes. Two deep, black pools that unleashed femininity, sweetness, capable of bewitching those who casually looked into them, brushing her with their glance. A small tattoo on her left wrist featured a tribal rose while her right ankle displayed a pink dolphin. She was a confirmed single at twenty-five, wanting only to have fun without tying herself to anyone. Up until then she had had only one important love story, which had lasted around two years. The madly in love sixteen-year old had been distraught and disillusioned when her boyfriend had broken up with her. From that time on, Francesca had decided on her priorities: studies, career, fulfillment in her work, a house that was all hers and maybe, someday, even her own business. She had really had fun during those three weeks on vacation. Shopping, excellent cooking, a few evenings at the discothèque or nightclubs, swimming, long, relaxing walks and wonderful views. There was no lack of friendships with the locals, like Dina, a nice old lady that lived along the road of shops and who, when she saw her passing by, invited her up to her small apartment for a cup of coffee and to talk about when she was young. Around noon, Francesca loved going out for an aperitif before lunch or else a nice fruit ice-cream. She preferred the mandarin and lemon flavors, in a cup. She slowly savored the ice cream, careful to not let it melt on her fingers, when it might end up on her dress. Sometimes, she enjoyed causing a little chaos by strolling along the path around the lake, in the most popular zone for swimmers, in skin-tight bathing suits that emphasized her beauty. She walked slowly, entertained by the infantile reactions of the men: some came out with foolish grins and stared at her with the vain hope of attracting her attention, others who pulled their stomachs in and posed like Greek statues and others yet whose comments on her shape were explicit, if not vulgar. Once, a not particularly young man made her laugh until her sides split; he stood in front of her in a position that was intended to be sexy and definitely was not. And if that wasn't enough, he had clumsily slipped some handkerchiefs inside his bathing suit hoping to increase his virility; the strategy failed miserably since he had exaggerated the dimensions, and small scraps of cloth peeped pitifully from the unforgiving suit. And, as if that itself wasn't enough, while he was trying to put on his most winning smile, unfortunately for him, the illusion was destroyed as his dentures fell noisily to the ground. Francesca was without a doubt very pleasing, and beyond the more or less consistent masculine admiration, she generated angry glares from the women who envied her sensual and elegant figure, her overflowing femininity and her impishly solar attitude, not to forget that she attracted the attention of their husbands or fiancés much more than they did. Many of them courted her during those days that she spent alone, but from the ranks of suitors, she had chosen only a lucky few, strictly those that she imagined would entertain her, in and out of a comfortable bed. She had casually had sex with the hotel's server and cook, several times and in the most absurd places: in the kitchen, in the cold storage and in the laundry-room. They were both very cute boys; the first was thirty years old and had his degree in engineering but, unable to find work, he earned a little money by working as a seasonal server. The cook wasn't even twenty yet. Other than these two, she had met a married, middle-aged man with three children in tow, who had tickled her fancy on the first day of her vacation. His hotel was only fifty meters from hers. She had set her eyes on him and seduced him with enchanting glances and smiles, sent his way with deliberate intensity, every time he looked her way. At first, he hadn't paid much attention, but then he quickly gave way to temptation. Not even four days after their first encounter he moved closer to get to know her at the first chance. That day, Francesca was sitting at one of the small tables outside a baroque-style bar. Wearing her sunglasses atop her head, she was staring fixedly at the lake while sipping from a goblet of pinot grigio. She had smiled when she saw him arrive and sit at a nearby table, knowing that her prey had fallen into the trap. She had finished drinking her wine while the man had continued to sit there without breathing. He pretended to look around, while casting a glance toward Francesca from time to time, but obviously knew neither how to move nor what he should do. Perhaps he was afraid of being discovered there by his wife, whom he had conveniently let go shopping with their children. He hadn't gone with them because he wasn't feeling well: that had been his excuse. Francesca had begun to stare at him, seeming to want to study the slightest details of his face, body even his most imperceptible movements. He had become aware of that scrupulous examination and had begun to move his right leg in a nervous tic. She smirked, and then stood up, took his hand and dragged him behind her. They had remained closed in the girl's room for an entire afternoon. Satisfied by the victory, she had spent the rest of the evening in a club where she had danced until dawn and from which she left completely drunk.

MOMENTS IN TIME

She was a very serious girl when she was at school or at home, obedient to the rules and strict with herself. However, when she was on vacation, free from all commitments and obligations, she liked to have fun, always prudent but without giving up some small transgressions. When having sex, she always took, and made her partners take, the necessary precautions. She was a health-freak, she loved sports, her family was fortunately well-off; in short, she lacked nothing and there, in that splendid spot, nestled among the mountains, the sun seemed to smile on her life, her career and on her radiant future. Francesca felt like she had the world at her fingertips! With her luggage ready for her departure, she sat in the hotel's bar savoring a fruit juice. Before leaving, though, she had decided to grant herself a last visit to the lake. She went and watched as the ducks splashed in the water. She wanted to go see the Piazza della Catena, splendid and majestic, along the lake's shore, with the imposing Baroque statue of St. John Nepomuceno. She had visited the town, up and down, but it still wasn't enough as she decided to take a last walk through the town, since she still had time to spare. So, she gave a last look at Piazza November III, at the majestic Pretorian Palace and at her favorite, the Church of the Inviolate. She adored its Baroque architectural style, the fascinating frescoes of the dome and the paintings guarded inside. Those places gave her a strange sensation, as though they hid a mysterious entity, a sort of magical presence.

Returning the way she had come, she walked along the path where some old oak trees danced in the wind. The knotted limbs seemed to bow before her as if in welcome. The pleasantly light aroma of lemons hung in the air. Then, she stopped again at the edge of the lake, where a clumsy boy bumped into her, one of the four young me she had seen arrive by a lateral path. They were Giorgio, Augusto, Lorenzo and Emanuele who were taking a stroll and fiddling around among themselves. When they saw her, they pushed Lorenzo against her, just to play a joke on their friend who, when he noticed her strolling on the beach, had said:

"Such a beautiful girl... wouldn't even notice someone like me!"

As soon as he realized he had hit her with his elbow, Lorenzo instinctively took Francesca by the arm to keep her from falling in the water. As he held her and repeatedly apologized, he continued to turn around and glare angrily at his friends for having caused him to make such a bad impression. As soon as his hand touched her skin, Francesca immediately felt a big tug at her heart, and a warm feeling that spread through her body, together with a sudden shiver. Her heart began to beat erratically, she was stunned and couldn't understand what was happening to her, but she turned and smiled at that boy who continued to hold her tight. Her heart was in her throat, she felt naked, completely undressed by her inner force; helpless, she could hardly breathe, as though there was no air. Her tanned skin camouflaged the blush that had appeared on her face. Those sensations were strange to her, never before felt: she couldn't react. This was so unlike her, to melt like ice cream in the sun, in front of a guy... Meanwhile, he had become purple and furious because of his friends' laughter. His eyes met hers for a moment, and Lorenzo remained speechless. Mamma mia, how embarrassing! He thought. Francesca, meanwhile, felt a terrible sense of panic, even though she didn't let on. The scene, which seemed to them to last forever, only lasted a few seconds. Then Lorenzo, abruptly turning around, waved goodbye, muttering "ciao" and started running toward his friends, who had already drifted off. When he reached them, everything ended in laughter, like always. Francesca, instead, stood there for several minutes before she realized she was alone.

FAMILY VACATION

Dawn's colors over the Trentino Mountains in high summer are so intense that they seem to be accompanied by the faintest of harmonies. Life begins to move in the eco of the first notes. It's not a rare thing, early in the morning, to run into a deer or someone carrying a backpack heading along one of the many paths while taking a long hike. At dawn, your sight is captivated by the mountains surrounding Val Campelle and by the first lights that glide like a paintbrush along the slopes up to the peaks almost imagining that they give them color and life. The impressive mountains almost seem like mothers as they surround and protect that alpine valley, their child. The cars begin their climb up the streets. The tourists and families arrive looking for peace, nature, relaxation and also a bit of fresh air: here, it feels like a dream where you can fill your lungs and be absorbed by nature's calm, after leaving the smothering heat of the cities. You can relax by hiking, chatting, stopping to sleep under the pines and even by visiting an Alpine hut or ecotourism to taste local products, typical of the Trentino zone. Here and there rocks, even very large ones, appear on the meadow where sitting and observing the panorama is usually a foregone action. A small fir tree is near one of these, hiding a small, single mushroom in its shadow: it's a porcini; it seems to have chosen that spot so it wouldn't be seen, as though it had no intention of being eaten. A light breeze tickles and nips at your face. Walking along the path that leads to a group of cabins, passing them and continuing toward the Five Cross Pass, it seems as though you can hear a stifled voice, perhaps a greeting from the fir trees as they move delicately and rhythmically, caressed by a light breeze. You can hear the roar of the river in the woods, wanting to be heard. Stones of various sizes and shapes roll in its clear waters, rumbling unsatisfied and tired, hoping to be able to stop, too, in one of the beds in that wonderful place. The water is freezing, because it began in one of the Alpine lakes found at two thousand meters above sea level.

Near a curve, a man who seems to be about one hundred years old, wearing a rough woolen shirt with large red and green squares, heavy pants, hiking boots and a traditional dark green felt cap, decorated with edelweiss and a small, dark grey feather, is sitting on an old tree trunk with a backpack over his shoulders. His face is marked by deep wrinkles – the wrinkles of a difficult life, lived right there in the mountains. But his complexion is red, and his blue eyes stand out like aquamarines set on ruby-red cloth. The man is smoking a pipe, distracted, and his ice-reflected eyes scan the countryside. He seems to be part of the panorama. He hears the sound of bells. Here and there cows busily eat the tasty fresh grass. They seem tired and bored, even when they lift their heads and seem to slowly look around, stopping once in a while when a person walks by and exchanges their gaze. Who knows if maybe the cows think, when they look at you, "Who is that funny human being watching us like that, as though they had never seen anyone eat before...?" With a sly, uncaring attitude towards those looking at them and anything else that might distract them too much from their morning meal they once again lower their heads to eat the fresh grass. There is also a small, cute calf – all black with ruffled hair - that continues moving, agitated, lowing loudly, trying to make its mother understand that it is still hungry and wants milk.

A finch, maybe as big as the palm of a hand, hops along the wooden windowsill searching for something to eat and every once in a while pecks at the glass in the window. Its chest feathers are a pinkish brown and the head a delicate blue. Its strident call penetrates the dreams even of those who are deeply asleep. The first timid light of dawn begins to creep along the walls, invading the bedroom. It drew closer to the objects in the dark and very slowly gave them colors; near the door, a painting of an Alpine sunset hung on the wall; to the side, a stand holding a couple of caps: one woolen, simple and black, the other purple with many flowers and animals on it. Some wrinkled clothes were strewn on the chairs. The sun paused for a few more seconds on the dresser; he also liked the clock set in the piece of inlaid wood, shaped like an Alpine hat. The hands showed seven o'clock a.m. Lorenzo turned over on his side, rubbing his eyes and looking at the time. Grumbling, he extended his arms and completely stretched, being careful not to awaken his wife. Watching her, he gave a hint of a content smile. They had made love that night; those whispers, the almost stifled words, the intense sighs and the moans, their bodies, warm and consumed with passion, the desired caresses, the sought-out heat, the odor of the flesh consumed by ardor and weakened in their embrace, mellowed, like a child fed on swollen breasts that finally settles down, cuddled in its mother's arms, waiting for sleep. She laid her head on his chest and he stroked her hair. Lorenzo had to get up, but waited a moment and looked at the sheets that created a harmonious fold around her body, around her generous figure. It was like a picture that he would like to have known to draw and, while his desire regained life after the restful night, the overbearing sound of the alarm clock broke into the scene. In half an hour they would have to get ready to go on an outing.

"Damn… what a racket this alarm clock makes!"

Lorenzo quietly exclaimed, immediately turning the diabolical device off, giving Francesca a few more minutes of sleep. He got up from the bed; it was cold that morning and being bare-chested and wearing only boxers, he quickly gathered up his clothes and put them on. Then he decided to go to the kitchen and prepare breakfast. He loved making coffee with its strong, decisive aroma. He had no idea why, but it gave him a sense of gratification. He slipped into his slippers and went downstairs, careful to not make them creak. They were made of wood, just like the rest of the cabin. He held onto the handrail because he was still half asleep and was afraid of tripping. In the kitchen, he looked out the window and saw the little bird and the beautiful sunny day waiting for him. It had rained some, sporadic summer thunderstorms that blew quickly over the mountain and left just as quickly, leaving behind the beautiful scent of wet grass and a clear sky. The three weeks of vacation had passed quickly and now there were only a couple of days before they had to leave. They had really gone all over, alternating days of complete relaxation with walks, playing with the girls and hiking in those marvelous spots. They went to see the lakes of Nassare and Stellune and many others, too, completely immersed in the pleasure of wandering around that paradise, reaching an intimate contact with the countryside, nature and themselves. That Friday they wanted to visit the refuge in Val Caldenave and eat lunch there. The plain was about 1700 meters above sea level; a crystal clear river winds through the center, its continuous curves designed like the movement of an enormous snake. Horses usually grazed there; an Alpine refuge dominated the area a number of yards above, where you could rest or eat some excellent dishes. Behind this, an enormous massif towers, vigilant, conferring the spot with the surrealistic feeling of being inside a refined painting. It was there that Lorenzo had rediscovered his serenity and had understood the importance of the time spent with his family. In the mountains, his days were timed by the sunrise and the sunset, without looking at clocks or running for the phone. The days had become grains of real life and together they had created the rock, the stone tablet, on which they inscribed their words and smiles, dreams and emotions forever.

In the mountains, the soul and the heart rediscover what they are, and reach for Heaven.

The coffee began to grumble in the coffee-maker as its aroma wafted through the room. Suddenly, he felt the soft touch of a warm hand running through his unkempt hair; this was followed by fingers delicately massaging his earlobes; the exploration concluded with a kiss on his cheek. Even though, through the years, it had become a morning habit, it was still caused a sense of pleasure that he exchanged with a delicate caress.

"Hi, sweetheart, good morning. Would you like a cup of coffee? Or would you prefer a glass of orange juice?"

"No, no, just give me a good cup of black coffee. I sure need it this morning, I just can't wake up!"

Lorenzo handed her the boiling hot cup, and then poured one for himself.

"So, did you sleep well?"

"Yes, sweetheart, very well. It must be the place or the air, but I really am sleeping very well."

She had been fascinated and impressed when she arrived, seeing those wonderful places, those mountain tops that seemed to be able to write in the sky, taking their ink from the clouds that surrounded them.

Francesca smiled and began drinking her coffee, strictly without sugar. Even though Lorenzo filled her with compliments, she knew perfectly well that her two pregnancies and her upcoming fortieth birthday had filled her out a little, and she didn't want to exacerbate the situation. She was happy, though, to have lost a few pounds during the vacation. The swimming she rarely did in the city and the healthy eating had put her back in shape, both in body, and especially, in her soul. She had been restored and felt great.

"Francesca, I'm going to go wake up the girls, now; meanwhile, enjoy your coffee in peace… You know, I think we should probably dress a little heavier for our hike."

"I think you're right, it looks really cold outside. I can hear the wind blowing and I'm pretty sure there was a big downfall, last night…"

"Yep. That's exactly what happened, dear."

He began climbing the stairs as he has answered his wife, and then opened the door to where his daughters were sleeping.

Going near the bed, he moved the curtains to let in the light. Carlotta immediately pulled the covers up over her face and turned over, mumbling.

"Good morning, Daddy!"

Ariel opened her eyes and greeted her father, twisting her mouth up for the usual kiss from her daddy that lit up her face. She adored being cuddled, especially by her daddy.

"Come on, girls, today we're going to go see the horses!"

"Okay, Daddy. You go on ahead… We're coming right away! We'll just stay in bed for five more minutes…"

Hearing her say that, he frowned, drawing close to her with a serious look on his face; he answered her as he kissed her on the forehead.

"Girls, I'm giving you five minutes, and I mean it; five minutes!"

After a few seconds, the little sisters, first one and then the other, pulled their knees up to their stomachs, holding them in place with their hands, and then suddenly letting them go like a spring; tossing off the covers, they began to laugh. They stayed on the bed, with their arms and legs stretched out, lifting their heads slightly so they could look out the window.

"I'm going downstairs. Are you coming?"

"Yes, yes… I'm coming. You go on ahead…"

"Okay, but don't make Daddy get mad, because I want to see the horses and the cows today…"

"I said yes, so go!"

Hearing her sister's peevish answer, Ariel stood up, put on her plush, cow-shaped slippers, went first into the bathroom and then downstairs for breakfast: the hot milk with chocolate cookies that she liked so much were waiting for her… she had also lost a few pounds and could therefore take advantage. She thought that sometimes her sister could be so unbearable; she was so rude when answering and she just couldn't stand it!

Carlotta showed up around twenty minutes later, her face still puffy with sleep, dragging along her black teddy bear Tiffy.

"Well, good morning, young lady; I was just coming upstairs to get you, you know? We're all waiting for you to organize the trip! Don't let it happen again!"

Eating her cookies at the table, Ariel turned red, shrugged her shoulders and giggled at her sister being scolded.

"But Mommy! I'm tired today; can I stay in bed and sleep a little longer?"

"No, today we're going on a trip to see the horses and then eat in a nice, new place. Don't be so naughty!"

"Oh, all right…"

Carlotta sat down, glared at her sister, who was still giggling and started eating breakfast. The sisters were five and six years old and had very different characters. Ariel, the oldest, was judicious, always smiling and enthusiastic to do or discover something new. She was completely dependent on her parents to dress her, to tie her shoes and to give her a bath. She was very affectionate, very close to her parents, whom she never disobeyed. She loved reading cartoons that talked about animals and fairies, pistachio ice cream and cheese. Just the opposite, Carlotta was often naughty. Unlike her sister she loved to be alone and play with her teddy bear. She also loved animals and nature. She stayed for hours looking at a meadow, contemplating a flower as it opened, admiring it. At times, she chatted animatedly for long periods with the flowers. She had already begun tying her shoes by herself, and would have liked to be autonomous in getting dressed or other things, except that sometimes she couldn't do it and this made her edgy and unhappy. Even though she didn't let on, she really loved being cuddled by her parents. They got their facial features from their father. Their eyes and mouth surely came from their mother; also their shoulder-length, intensely brilliant black hair. Ariel was a little taller than Carlotta, but they were both pleasingly plump. When they smiled, their faces filled with the light and sweetness typical of children. Beyond that, the few missing teeth, evident in both of their smiles, could only transmit the same cheerfulness to those looking at them.

They left around nine. They took the hydrogen-propelled family car, the only type allowed by the London Agreement of 2018 that imposed that only that type of fuel could be used for motor vehicles, and headed toward the Bridge of Conseria, the referral point found just a few kilometers from their cabin. Once there, they put on their backpacks and took the uphill path, with the Malga Caldenave as their set destination. After about three hours spent on a spectacular visit, they returned to the car. The trip had been exhausting, but truly beautiful. They had also met Enzo, a local inhabitant, who had a ranch not far away in the valley and was taking some of his clients on an excursion on horseback. The girls had obviously gone nuts when they saw the horses. They had also seen a lot of squirrels, a few cows, ponds and flowers. They were tired, but it had been worth it.

"Hey girls, do we want to go see Ralf?" asked Lorenzo as he loaded up the backpacks and gave the girls dry tee-shirts to put on.

"Yeeees!"

Francesca and Lorenzo had met Ralf one afternoon, thanks to the vivaciousness of his son, Victor, who had become friends with Ariel and Carlotta. All three of them had let themselves go for hours, playing on the swings and the slide. As a result, the boy's father, Ralf, had become friends with their parents. He was an entertaining, straightforward person. It was impossible to not notice his hair: lots of bright-red curls. His companion, Ana Paula, a native Brazilian, was also there with him. They had met while she was on vacation in Trentino. Everything had happened in the locale managed by Ralf, located on a gorgeous Alpine passage, the Manghen Pass. She had stopped for a bite with some friends, then to go on to the vault of Cavalese to visit the Fiemme Valley. When they had finished eating, her friends had gone away, but Ana Paula would never leave again. She was a famous lawyer in Sao Paulo and was ten years older than Ralf, but she had given up everything for that boy with the curly red hair.

Carlotta honked the horn, entertained, "Well, Daddy, shall we get a move on?"

"Yes, sweetheart, we're leaving now. Be patient a minute while we change Ariel's shoes, too, and then we'll go.

27

Lorenzo bent over and began to tie his daughter's shoes.

"Carlotta, get down from there, because now I have to get in."

"Ah, Mamma… Are you driving?"

"Yes."

"Oh, really?" Lorenzo asked, surprised.

"Yes, come on, love, let me drive the new car; I haven't driven it since we bought it."

"All right, but then you're driving home on Sunday, too, so I can enjoy the view during the trip without having to stress out about the road. Okay?

"Sold! That's good for me!"

Smiling, Francesca got into the driver's seat. Lorenzo was very jealous of his car. Every once in a while he told Francesca she didn't know how to drive and which irritated her immensely. So, when they quarreled, the subject came up sooner or later, and became a reason for greater tension and further arguments. They all climbed aboard and left for the vault of Manghen Pass. The children were enthusiastic at the idea of seeing their friend Victor again.

"By the way, Lorenzo, have you had that nightmare you told me about, again?" Francesca whispered to her husband as he sat next to her, looking out at the road.

"Yes. I woke up again last night with a start because of that usual dream, the same place I always see. The room with the white walls, a cross and a watch, but I don't know where I am. At first, I see a really bright light, then everything gets dark and suddenly, the lights are back. I hear voices, but I don't know who they are or what they are saying. There's a person in front of me; it's a girl, she stares at me, but I don't know who she is. She just stands there, motionless, looking at me. Then, I see a really strong light and suddenly, I see a huge green meadow with flowers that form a word, but I can't decipher it. Then, I see two figures: they seem to be an adult and a child who look and point at me. Suddenly, everything goes dark, I hear screaming, and I wake up."
"If you ask me, you should go see someone. This nightmare has been going on for a long time."

"Don't be silly!" he responded in annoyance.

"Whatever; I just hope it doesn't become a problem. We already have too many."

Francesca was hurt by her husband's sharp answer.

Lorenzo remained serious with a worried look, and then turned angrily to look out the window at the panorama. They argued and quarreled at times, even about useless things. But, in the end, he understood that she was only worried about him and about how lucky he was to have found her and that such a beautiful, sweet and intelligent woman could be so in love with him, with all the other men around. As he meditated on this, he remembered their first date, the first time they had made love.

TOGETHER

When he returned home from the vacation spent with his friends at Riva del Garda, Lorenzo put his heart into it and graduated that same year in Mechanical Engineering. It was November 15, 2008. A little more than a month later, on Christmas Eve, his girlfriend left him because she had to move with her Family to Germany for work. She didn't want a long-distance relationship and neither did he. Unfortunately, a severe financial crisis hit shortly after, bringing strong repercussions on a global level. So, because the job situation wasn't very shining in Trentino, either, he sent his CV out everywhere – even outside his own region – once he graduated, without getting discouraged; he had very little hope of being hired by one of the companies where, just a short while ago, he had thought he would accepted with wide-open arms. However, a few months later a technical office in Trento called him in for an apprenticeship. He considered this to be a transitory experience, while waiting for something better. Instead, he liked the job and learned so quickly that the owner, a very discerning person who understood his potential, other than teaching him the tricks of the trade, recommended him to their associates in Emilia Romagna where someday he would surely be put to better use and gain more personal satisfaction. So, a couple of years later, in the month of March, he received an important phone call from Bologna. Lorenzo was surprised by the call but also pleased by what they told him. The speaker gave a brief presentation, and then told him very succinctly that they wanted to meet him, the next day, if possible, to offer him a job in their work group concerned with research and development in the county seat of Felsineo. Overcome with enthusiasm, Lorenzo impulsively agreed to meet him the following day. After hanging up the phone, he suddenly realized that perhaps he had been a little too hurried. Even though it was a very important professional opportunity, he actually liked working where he was, he was near home, he got along well with his colleagues and lately was receiving a very decent salary. He was uncertain, torn by indecision and anxiety. After a few minutes he thought of calling his boss to explain what had happened and to maybe get some advice. He already knew, because his partners had informed him, and told Lorenzo that he had done the right thing in accepting that interview. He had to think about his career, his life. He really appreciated the call from Lorenzo. The following day, he woke up early, took a very hot shower, shaved carefully, put on his best suit, said a quick good-bye to his parents and drove the car to his appointment, armed with good will and hope, but also with a little touch of fear. When he arrived at the front of the company, he noticed that the huge building seemed like it was just built. He entered the lobby and started up the wide stairway. He followed the arrows that indicated various offices and their relative occupants. The name of the person who had contacted him on the phone was also there. He went up to the indicated floor and went to the door where "enter without knocking" was written in very large letters; he took a very deep breath and walked in. A woman was seated in front of him, behind a small desk. She was very thin, with a worried, anxious look on her face. Isabella had been a secretary for just a few months and lived in constant fear of being fired; she was around forty years old, her blond hair was tied back, her glasses were very thick with a black plastic frame, her strict stare a perfect match to her severely-cut blue suit. Lorenzo timidly gave her his name and told her why he was there. She looked him up and told him to "have a seat" as she picked up the phone and informed the director of his arrival. Lorenzo thought that if she didn't like him already, who knew what the personnel director waiting for him would think. When he was called and went into the room he was so tense that he stared fixedly at a spot on the wall, near a reproduction of a painting by Magritte. He stared at the painting for so long that the director seated in front of him couldn't help ribbing him by saying, "If you like it so much you can take it home with you!" The room was bare and very Spartan, with a laptop and a few scattered documents on top of a very large desk. The man was seated behind it, without a tie and in his shirtsleeves. He hadn't reached forty yet and, squinting a little, he studied this boy from Trento, not much younger than himself, serious and concentrated as though he would jump to attention at the first sign of command. He had already studied his curriculum and called the office in Trento to ask for information from his partner. Lorenzo was in a cold, agitated sweat and didn't know where to look while waiting for the man to ask him something. Sitting there with his legs crossed, wearing a tie and jacket, he probably didn't even realize that he wasn't wearing socks. The personnel director smiled. Lorenzo, on the other hand, turned purple. He wanted to disappear. Right then, the director, taking a peek at his records, began asking him questions. It was over very quickly. He moved to Bologna the following week and began an internship that lasted several months. He learned the new technologies that during those years were in a phase of heavy expansion and that were being developed and studied in that company. Everything took off from discoveries made by the CERN. Having seen the capabilities that Lorenzo had demonstrated, he was soon sent to the branch in Padua, where an experimental phase was in progress on new alloys that could be applied in the aerospace industry. Lorenzo was enthusiastic about the idea because it gave him the chance to participate in an important project. Who would have ever thought! It was September 16, 2012. He was already in Padua on September 18, in an apartment that the company had provided. That day, the first in that new city, he thought he would like to celebrate with a good booze-up and share that special moment with his old friends, with whom he only exchanged holiday greetings by texting and a few sporadic phone calls. But, it wasn't possible. Their friendship was still very much alive and heartfelt; however, their life's journey had divided them. And so, alone in a new city he would just have to celebrate by chatting with himself. As he walked out the front door of his new house, he was knocked to the sidewalk by a woman walking swiftly past. She wore tight jeans and a lovely, tight-fitting deep purple pullover. He instinctively apologized, even though she had pushed him down. That woman, who already had continued on her way, stopped abruptly several yards ahead. Francesca turned around. That voice paralyzed her once again. Once again she felt herself falling into a state of helplessness, of total confusion. Her heart began to beat rapidly, as it had so long ago. But this time, even though intimidated by that gorgeous woman, he drew closer to her with a slight smile.

"Hey, uh, ciao...forgive me, please."

She stood there, staring at him in silence.

"Excuse me; you know...uh, I didn't see you coming, really."

She silently nodded in response, but was still unable to say a word.

"If you could, uh, perhaps, forgive me."

She smiled.

I was saying, if uhm, you could forgive me, uh...I'll buy you a drink!"

She nodded her agreement and answered with a trembling thread of her voice "Okay, let's go."

The company of a girl right then was just what the doctor ordered, so he wouldn't have to celebrate alone. She was still confused, though, she felt like she was dying from the excitement, but she didn't let him see. She was very much touched by the fact that fate had let her meet that boy again, right there in her own city.

A red light on Via Venezia, in the center of Padua. They had already been going out for a couple of weeks over the weekends, and they were in contact with messages or phone calls in the evening. The city was revealing itself to be indeed splendid and fascinating. Monuments, churches, incredible plazas, not to forget the wonderful bars where life abounded, thanks also to the university that attracted students from all over the world. And he had a tour-guide par excellence, a truly inexhaustible source of information on anything he wanted to know. They were both art enthusiasts, especially for medieval art. That day they were going to visit the Basilica of Saint Anthony and the Scrovegni Chapel, an extraordinary work of frescoes by Giotto. Building sites popped up just about everywhere; workers could be seen on every corner. The city was once flourishing, as were the residents, who enthusiastically participated more and more in this rebirth. A project for giving more value to the entire city was in progress. In addition to the restoration and the requalification of the buildings in the historical center, the population was centering its attention on alternative energy so as to become independent on an energy level, thanks to photoelectric fields and the new solar and geothermic technologies.

The light turned green; Lorenzo suddenly twisted around in his seat and, boosting his courage, said "it's now or never"; he looked at Francesca, took a deep breath and kissed her. It was done impulsively, hastily, he certainly hadn't thought he could do it; he overcame his shyness for the first time by doing such a thing, but he just couldn't wait anymore: he had wanted to do it for so long it was suffocating him. The horns around them continued to honk while they continued kissing. After a few seconds, they realized it would be a good idea to move; they smiled and took off. Lorenzo couldn't believe he had done it, that he had actually had the courage · to do it. He was incredulous, but happy. Francesca was trying to breathe normally after that emotional upheaval. That day marked the beginning of their story.

Their first trip together was to Trieste. Several months after their engagement, they finally had a week of vacation, ideal for carving out a moment for intimacy among their many obligations. Even Francesca worked a lot; she had been an executive in her father's company. This was a week just for them. They arrived in the city on Monday and, as the taxi driver who had accompanied them to their hotel had suggested, they had gone to the busiest street in the city to take a stroll. There were indeed many shops and they were impressed by the numerous ice cream parlors. Unable to resist, they wandered around with two colorful, gigantic ice cream cones just to fall into the sacrosanct dimension of vacations. Later, under the starry sky and hot air, they strolled along the promenade. They walked hand in hand, up to the peak of "lover's lane" where they exchanged kisses and caresses. Then, back at the hotel, exhausted, they fell into the sweetness of a deep sleep. The following day they walked nonchalantly around Trieste, their curiosity piqued by the many plazas and fountains, especially the one with the Tritons. Considering the very sunny day, they decided to visit the Miramar Castle and surrounding park, referred to them as not-to-be-missed beauties by a couple of friends who had been there just a month previous while on their honeymoon in the selfsame city. Arriving at the park in just a few minutes they were surprised by the multitude of plants of every kind that enlivened the interior. The whole place was perfect, clean and well-taken care of. Among the various attractions, there were greenhouses that protected an almost enchanted environment. Thousands of colors brushed the air, thousands of butterflies and hummingbirds of every kind carried Francesca and Lorenzo into a magical world. It was the first time they had seen hummingbirds and they were stunned. After walking around the park, they went in to visit the castle. The rooms, maintained in absolute authenticity, still had original furniture and tapestries from the eighteen hundreds. They visited each room meticulously browsing among porcelain vases, paintings, sculptures and every object that could carry them far back in time. Going out, they were blinded for a moment by the sun shimmering on the sea, but their sight returned immediately to unveil the wonders of a beautiful garden, with a small private port that the Hapsburgs had used to dock their boats. A representation of a sphinx over-looked the wharf, a life-sized statue that seemed to be put there to watch the sea and whoever drew near the castle. They suddenly realized that while they had been wandering around, it had grown quite late; the visitors were quickly exiting from the building as closing time drew closer. Before leaving, though, the two love-birds found their way back to the bedroom of the archduke Maximillian of Hapsburg. They read there that the archduke had lived there with his beloved wife, Carlotta of Belgium. It was just a moment; they were overcome by a wave of desire and passion. Giving a quick look around and finding themselves alone, they leaned against a column and began kissing each other voraciously. Francesca's hands clutched Lorenzo, who began to push against her sides, lifting her skirt with the palm of his hand. Right then, with a discreet cough, someone let them know he was there. Embarrassed and entertained at having been caught in the act, they left immediately. Back in the city, around seven o'clock in the evening and starving, they stopped in a restaurant. They had been so in awe of the castle they hadn't noticed that the day had flown by without them having eaten a bite of food. They were in a delightful little place. They gazed into each other's eyes from time to time as they ate. They had bought a bottle of red wine to accompany the food, which seemed an aphrodisiac to them. Between smiles and jokes, the evening was slipping away: they were there together and nothing else mattered. After paying the bill and leaving a generous tip, they returned to the hotel. Saying good night to the porter, who was always very nice, they stepped into the elevator. Lorenzo dropped his keys on the way up to the fifth floor, where their room was. Bending down at the same time to pick them up, they butted each other in the head. They both stood up, rubbing their heads, and laughed. Abruptly, Lorenzo turned serious, touched Francesca's hair and gazed into her eyes. She turned completely red. He pulled her close and kissed her. They began stripping without worrying about tearing their clothes. Francesca pushed stop and the elevator blocked. They made love then and there. When they had finished, they decided to continue going up and finishing their effusions in their room. Once dressed as well as possible, they arrived at their floor disheveled and flushed. As the door opened, they saw an elderly woman standing there, grumbling, in front of them. She was at least seventy, about five feet tall and wearing a long, nut-brown cotton jacket which blended in with her. She had a red and white polka-dot hat; her face was wrinkled and serious. She had been waiting for at least ten minutes. When she saw the couple, first she reprimanded them with a serious, frowning look and then, looking at them better, understood what they had just done and laughed. They reached their room laughing, and spent the rest of the week there, among those four walls, wrapped up in their passion.

MANGHEN PASS

A few curves later Lorenzo, staring out the window and his right hand clutching the door, said to his wife, "Be careful Francesca; honk when we reach the curves and go a little slower."

"Lorenzo, stop it, please! Don't make me raise my voice with the girls here."

"Okay, you're right. But at least honk in case cars come; the road is narrow!"

Snorting and rolling her eyes, she didn't answer him.

"C'mon Daddy, let's sing the mountain songs," said Ariel.

"Okay, let's go: 'when we will be out, out in the Valsugana...'"

And everyone sang it merrily, over and over again.

Lorenzo, native of a small town of the area, was happy that his daughters loved the land and its traditions so much.

"Shall we stop and get something to drink? We still have twenty minutes to go and I have to go to the bathroom."

"Okay, let's stop here. Look, there's a bar."

They were traveling along the road leading to Manghen Pass, near the town of Telve. A small stop was what they needed, so they went into the bar. They immediately noticed that it was quite attractive, well cared-for and clean, all in carved wood. Behind the counter, on which was written, "Look but Don't Touch", were two pretty girls, the sisters Fausta and Rosy, owners of the bar together with their brother and parents. They didn't seem related though because they didn't resemble each other. One was blonde, with big blue eyes, plump with a generous breast, while the other had brassy red hair, small green eyes, fairly thin and lacking curves. However, they both had big, welcoming smiles.

"I'm going to the bathroom; do you girls need to go?"

"No, no, Daddy. Go… Go, go!"

Lorenzo looked for directions for the restroom and disappeared. Francesca and the girls waited a few minutes and ordered when he returned

"An aperitif, a Veneto, please, and three fruit juices; the flavor doesn't matter."

"Well, it's a good thing I'm driving!" Francesca exclaimed.

"It certainly is, dear. In fact, I'm having alcohol to forget that you're driving."

"Here you go, sir," said Fausta, exhibiting her charms while bending over to hand him his glass.

Lorenzo smiled. Francesca frowned a moment and then said, "Well, look there in center because you won't see anything else until tomorrow!"

"Come on dear, I didn't even notice…"

While the two of them argued, the other customers in the bar had a laugh or two watching the squabble. Two elderly men leaning on the bar, drinking a glass of white wine, were particularly amused. The scene must have been a pleasant diversion to their everyday life, their usual discussions about work, on the pastures and mountains, subjects that often generated endless quarrels about trifles. Marital squabbles entertained them because they brought back memories of bygone days, when they were young and quarreled with their wives, a tradition that, however, they didn't mind still respecting even though many years of marriage had already gone by. One of the two wore a dark grey cap, typical of the shepherds of the area. His cheeks were slightly purple and his face was marked by time and weather; his long, grey beard was lightly stained yellow by tobacco. The men drank down their wine with a couple of sips and then went outside to smoke a cigarette.

"Yeah, yeah…" he said, smiling.

"Are we leaving?" the girls asked, tugging Lorenzo by the arm after drinking their juice.

"Yes, we're leaving now, but go slowly, girls."

They paid and left. After only twenty minutes they were already on the twelve curves that would take them to their destination.

"Look at that view!" said Francesca. "It's spectacular!"

"Yes, you're right," Lorenzo replied.

The girls were silent, their mouths hanging wide open.

"Mamma, Mamma, look…What are those white things moving around over there in front of us?" Carlotta asked.

"Girls, those are sheep."

"How cuuuute!" their daughters yelled.

They could see the flock very well, spread out over the pasture a little above where they were. They were quickly drawing closer, since they were along the road that they were following.

"Ugh," Francesca said, braking. Lorenzo looked at her, perplexed.

On the last curve, an enormous donkey stood stock still, in the middle of the road. It looked like a statue.

"C'mon, get out and make it go away."

"Are you crazy? Who can make it move?!"

"Get out! C'mon!"

"All right, I'll get out, but stay calm, because this won't be an easy job."

Lorenzo got out and walked near the donkey; the girls followed him excited and enthusiastic.

"Girls, please, stay away from here, because he might start kicking."

But the girls had already changed direction and were walking toward the flock. They pet a sheep with a lamb and Francesca had fun watching them.

"Mamma, look how pretty!"

"Yes, girls, but be careful not to hurt the lamb; he's like a little baby…"

"C'mon, move! C'mon, I'm hungry… Don't be like that, just move a little bit over that way, near your friends," Lorenzo said to the donkey in a friendly voice. But, it didn't give any sign of moving.

"C'mon, look… I'll make you move!"

He tried pushing it, but there was nothing doing; it seemed made of stone.

"It's impossible that no one is around, the shepherd or something…!"

In the distance, Francesca and the girls watched on, entertained by Lorenzo gesturing and talking to the donkey.

"Here I am… I'm coming!" said a young man. It was the shepherd, who was laughing as he ran down a nearby slope.

"Oh, thank goodness! C'mon, can you move this enormous donkey for me?"

"Yes, okay, I'll do it."

The shepherd whistled and a dog named Fido came running; he was all black, with long hair. The shepherd motioned with his hand for him to move the donkey and, in fact, at the second whistle, the donkey lowered its head very, very slowly, beginning to move toward the side of the street.

"Daddy, did you see that a pretty dog?" In the meantime, the girls had reached their father.

"Yes, Carlotta, I did. You know, sheep dogs are very obedient; they live with their owners for many months here in the mountains. They become friends, and love them. And, they help them in their work."

While they pet the dog, the shepherd whistled and the dog quickly ran to meet him; the shepherd had moved as quietly as a shadow to go and control his flock from a huge boulder that overlooked the area.

"Look!" Yelling and jumping with excitement, the girls pointed to a group of donkeys in the middle of the sheep. One of them had a sort of green blanket on its back with a big pocket in which they could see a small lamb.

"Daddy, Mommy, look…"

"A donkey has a little lamb in its pocket! Whose is it?"

Lorenzo explained to them that sometimes they put the little lambs in the donkeys' saddle bags when they transferred the flock.

"So, the donkey is the little lamb's papa… is it the donkey's now?" Ariel asked, smiling up at her father.

"No, Ariel, their mamma is still in the flock; they are moving to another area, soon. But, let's go now, because I'm hungry. Aren't you?"

"Yes, okay, Daddy, let's go, let's go! We're hungry, too!"

Francesca was already in the car. Five minutes after taking off, they were already at the restaurant, a fantastic spot that left them breathless, near the mountain peaks. Looking down, they could see the surrounding valleys.

"It's awe-inspiring…" Francesca said as she got out of the car.

Looking around, Lorenzo remembered when he and his friends went to these places on hiking excursions to the peaks when they were children many years before.

"Wow! Nothing has changed! It seems that time has stood still!"

The restaurant was near a small pond with which it formed a truly enchanting framework. Everyone noticed that there was complete chaos inside due to the ferment generated by passing tourists, bikers and cyclists. There was a very old man among the latter, dressed completely in yellow, with a bright bandana on which was written "Pirate". He had to have been very good to ride so far up on his bicycle!

Ana Paula saw them and went up to meet them with her usual cordial smile.

"Welcome! I kept you a table; come with me."

They went outside and sat down.

"What shall I bring you?"

"Well, what would you suggest?" asked Francesca.

"I would start with a nice plate of hors d'oeuvres … various salamis, cheese and others. Then I would suggest spetzlis with melted butter and speck, or a good goulash, but also some polenta with frankfurters and sausage. For dessert, I suggest the special cake of the house, a delight made with blueberries and wild strawberries."

"Do you want us to explode? Anyway, if it's all right with everyone else, it's okay with me. What do you two say? And Lorenzo?"

"Yes, yes, Mommy! Are there fried potatoes, too? And ice cream?" replied Carlotta.

"See," said Ana Paula, smiling and turning to Francesca, "here's someone who certainly has no problems!" And then, turning to go away with the order written on a scrap of paper, she finished aloud, "So then, fried potatoes for the girls!"

Everyone smiled and the girls seemed very excited. Meanwhile Francesca, already feeling guilty, searched for a perfect alibi for enjoying the caloric dishes that were about to arrive in peace: "It's one of our last meals, guys... so let's make this effort happily no? Even if I doubt we can finish everything..."

Lorenzo started to laugh and winked at the girls, "We can do it, we can do it... what do you girls say?"

Once lunch was over, Ariel and Carlotta ran to play with Victor. Most of the people were going away, so Ralf and Ana Paula stopped to talk with Lorenzo and Francesca. While the husbands talked about the mountains, the magical places surrounding them and excursions taken in the past, the wives talked about the goulash, with Francesca taking precise notes on the recipe; she could hardly wait to put the tasty dish to the test once they returned to Padua. As they spoke, the women never took their eyes off the children as they played wildly. At one point a handsome young man with tanned skin exited the restaurant. He sat down on a bench, leaning his back against the wall, and lit a cigarette.

"Who's the hunk?" Francesca asked, smiling at Ana Paula.

"It's my brother, Carlos. He gives a hand in the kitchen. Would you like to meet him?" her Brazilian friend answered, not without a touch of mischief.

"No, no, please! I was just joking. I'm not interested... c'mon, I'm married! He certainly is a good-looking boy, your brother and... taking a closer look...yes, yes, he looks a lot like you!"

"He's the family heartbreaker! I think he'll stay here, too; he doesn't seem too anxious to return to Brazil. He's a real whiz in the kitchen and he really likes working here. I'd be very happy to keep him near! He started out playing at being the assistant chef, but then he developed a passion for it and has become very good. He works long hours, but he's holding on tight..."

Suddenly, a man around forty years old came up the path, wearing a green bandana around his head, sunglasses, a small backpack, shorts and colored tee-shirt with "Ac\DC", the mythical hard rock group, written on it in garish colors. Lorenzo studied him closely, stood up and went toward him.

"Excuse me, are you Mario?"

"Yes, I am. Do we know each other?"

"I'm Lorenzo; c'mon, don't you recognize me? We went on a lot of excursions here around the Lagorai with all of our other friends! Pike's Peak, Stellune Lake or that time we went to the "lower lakes" where we stayed two days partying? C'mon, don't you remember?"

"Of course! Lorenzo! Now I remember you! So much time! What have you done since then?"

They hugged and began slapping each other warmly on the back.

"Now I live in Veneto; I come to Trentino on vacation. I moved to Padua for work and got married. I'm here on vacation with

48

my family." As he spoke, Lorenzo pointed to his wife, and then his daughters who were skipping nearby.

"Well done! C'mon, let's drink a nice grappa to celebrate!"

"Yes, a grappa is just what we need, for digesting, too... eating here is like Heaven; you just can't resist the temptation."

"I can see that, dear Lorenzo, you've put on a few pounds, too! What do you want, time passes for everyone, but the important thing is to stay well, and you seem to be doing just fine!" While he spoke, Mario continued to tap his friend's stomach.

They sat down at the table and Mario ordered two "Cornelian" grappas.

"Are you married? Are you here alone?"

"Yes, I'm here alone; I took a quick walk, about half an hour, just to loosen up my legs. Nothing special. I'm not married, but I have a partner who is working today. You know, she's a clerk, and I just couldn't resist all this... such a beautiful day! I see that you, on the other hand, have a beautiful family!" Mario finished with an eloquent wink.

"I'm not complaining; Francesca and I both have good jobs, good daughters, even if they're a little rambunctious... but I consider myself a very lucky man."

"Well done! I see that you found yourself a very beautiful woman! You can introduce me to them later, but now, let's drink to them!"

Finishing the grappa, they exchanged a few more words, then stood up and headed toward Francesca. Mario introduced himself and while he shook her hand, he stood enchanted for a few seconds by that woman with her deep black eyes, streaked by splendid purple highlights magically created by the sunlight. When the introductions were made, Mario invited the entire family to a festival that he was on his way to. Since the place was on their way back to the cabin, they accepted happily. They affectionately said good-bye to their friends and left, following Mario's car. Just before reaching the valley they turned in the direction of a town that was on a marvelous, small plain and wound their way a little way up a slope.

Look, Daddy, there's a sign with a big 'P'."

"You're right, Ariel. That sign means we are near our destination. Those big 'P's mean that there's a parking lot and probably for the party!"

The children smiled and Lorenzo parked the car. Meanwhile, Mario waited for the family, "Girls, are you ready?"

They gave a resounding chorus of "Yes".

"Okay then, let's go see what's going on!"

"Lorenzo, look!" Francesca said, smiling widely.

Lorenzo opened his eyes up wide. Along the way up to the party he saw craftsmen that were giving demonstrations of various ancient trades: the blacksmith, who pounded a piece of incandescent iron, someone weaving baskets or making "scandole", wooden tiles completely hand-made, with slits, with which the Alpine cabins were covered. They were all fascinated, especially the girls, at seeing the skills of these people who did all they could to show a past that was still present, thanks to them, people who were proud of their origins and traditions.

"Mommy," Ariel asked, "do these people really do these beautiful things?"

"No, sweetheart. It's a demonstration of how hard they used to work to get things that we can get much easier now, thanks to technology. But, it's also important to understand that certain traditions are never forgotten."

"That's right, girls," Lorenzo added, "history is important: you should never forget where we came from, who we are or our origins. We should treasure them."

"Okay, Daddy, but these people are so old and they still know how to do these crafts… and, is fabric still made that way?"

Carlotta had topped in front of a woman who was weaving linen and pointed at her, perplexed.

The woman laughed along with the others at the innocent question; then, Lorenzo answered his daughter, "No, Carlotta, they are only giving a demonstration; they're very good exactly because they have known how to keep the tradition of the old crafts alive throughout the years. Now they don't do these works anymore…"

Then he whispered in her ear, "Anyway, you don't point your finger at people… it's bad manners!"

Lorenzo took the child by the hand and continued walking. The road continued on for about one hundred meters, and every twenty meters there was a spot where these demonstrations took place. As a whole, already picturesque on its own, was submerged in a forest of chestnuts, birches and pines.

"Here we are!" Mario said.

At the end of the Handicrafts Path (which was written on the sign indicating the small show) they saw a large clearing being used for the festival and overlooked by the ruins of a castle that they discovered was called High Castle.

"Wow! This is a medieval festival!" Francesca exclaimed.

"Yes, it's a firm tradition by now. All of the organizers, waiters, musicians and cooks dress up in period clothing. Even the dishes are cooked according to the ancient recipes."

"Mamma mia, how cool is this! I didn't know there was such a festival here! It's too bad I'm not hungry anymore, I'm curious about all those strange-looking dishes! Lorenzo, look how good they were; it seems like we're really in the medieval period. What beautiful costumes!"

Francesca felt very well indeed; that festival seemed like the cherry on top of the unforgettable vacation cake. She was surprised to see Ana Paula and her brother show up, but they sat at a table where other friends were waiting for them. Her husband had stayed at home with their son because he felt exhausted that evening. They greeted each other quickly with the promise to meet up afterwards. The music began as the sky darkened. They played medieval pieces where the flute and the delicate-sounding harp reigned. They created the ideal frame in that context, where you expected to see a knight or princess appear at any moment. When the concert was over and everyone had been much applauded, a very young boy playing an accordion took their place. After meticulously preparing himself he began tapping his foot in rhythm on the ground, and then masterfully played several cheerful, popular dances.

"Lorenzo, come dance with me."

"I don't really feel like it…"

"Oh, you're always the same! And listen how beautiful it is!" Francesca exclaimed, a little annoyed by her husband's behavior.

"Oh, all right… but just one, okay?!"

And he danced that dance, even though against his will, to give in to his wife who had insisted so much. Francesca wanted to dance another, but he didn't want to hear about it. It was then that Mario came up to Francesca, bowing in a style worthy of the period they were celebrating, and offering his hand, he inquired, "Milady, will you do me the honor of conceding me this dance?"

"Certainly," she answered as the whole family laughed at the old-fashioned invitation made so clumsily. Mario was likeable and entertaining and the girls adored him, even though they were quickly falling asleep because of the long, exhausting day.

Lorenzo noticed this and told Francesca that it would be best if they left.

They took their leave of Mario and headed toward Ana Paula to say good-bye before they left. They had seen her arrive with her brother, probably to dance a little before going home.

While they were saying good-bye, a slow dance began to play. Carlos stood up smiling, took Francesca by the hand and dragged her onto the dance floor.

"I'll take a last dance," she said, entertained, while she let the young man guide.

"Sure, go ahead!" Lorenzo replied, sitting down with the girls, to talk with Ana Paula.

"You're really beautiful, you know," said Carlos, looking Francesca straight in the eyes, wickedly.

"Thank you, Carlos."

"If you want I'll come up to the mountain tonight; I know where you are staying, and we can meet in the woods..."

"What in the world are you thinking?!" Francesca replied, embarrassed.

"Well, I saw how you were looking at me!"

While saying this latter, Carlos slid his right hand delicately from Francesca's side to her rear.

"If you don't move your hand from there, immediately, you will get my knee between your legs so hard that you won't try that again with a woman for a very long time! Have I made myself clear?"

Francesca has spoken very calmly while giving her most cordial smile; Carlos showed that he had received her message by withdrawing his hand.

"Excuse me," he said, "I misunderstood."

"I certainly agree!"

The misunderstanding ended there; the exhausted family took off for the cabin, with the children sound asleep on the back seat of the car.

Returning down toward the valley, they admired, perhaps for the first time; the evening panorama, with all the lights on, made the Valsugana a sort of starry sky on the ground. They then began the rise leading to their cabin in the Val Campelle. Everyone was so tired that they all went to bed.

"Good night, my love," Francesca said.

"Night," Lorenzo replied, hugging his wife as she fell asleep in just a few moments.

He had seen the whole dance scene out of the corner of his eye and was happy to love a woman who couldn't be seduced even by such a handsome, attractive man. Yes, he was indeed very lucky. Then, he started thinking about the past and when he was about to make the biggest mistake of his life, a mistake that he had avoided by pure chance but had made him realize just how much he really loved his woman. Even at a distance of many years the mere thought of how he could have lost her made him suffer terribly and he still couldn't forgive himself for his weakness.

THE TEMPTATION

They had been married just a short time and were very happy.
They had decided to go to Francesca's place of origin,
Calabria, for their summer vacation. They left at the beginning
of August from Verona's airport. After boarding, they sat next to
each other, hand-in-hand. They were met in Reggio Calabria by
Francesca's aunt and uncle, Annalisa and Carmelo, two
infinitely cordial people who treated their guests with great
care. It was Lorenzo's first visit to southern Italy. He had
visited several zones on the peninsula, but the closest place to
the "boot's toe" he had been to was Velletri, in Lazio. They
accommodated them in an apartment belonging to Francesca's
parents, which was usually rented out to tourists, considering
how little they used it. They found it quaint and very
comfortable, a simple, Spartan-style room about sixty square
feet. There was a lovely terrace on the roof, all for them; they
could lie in the sun and on the canary yellow with red stripes
lounge chairs. They could see the Messina Straits from there,
which made them want to visit the island. Their passion for art
and history pushed them towards Palermo, Catania, Messina,
Noto and all those places that sheltered the great treasures of
the past. From the cathedrals, to the Baroque palaces, to the
monuments that testified as to how many civilizations had
contaminated the island, everything was wrapped up in
enchantment. Traces and testimonies of the ancient world:
Greek, Roman, Norman, Arabic, Spanish; they were visible

everywhere. The mixing-up of the styles struck them deep in their souls. So, Lorenzo and Francesca didn't let the opportunity to disembark in Sicily pass by and they feasted their eyes on those fairy-tale panoramas, architectural splendors of enormous beauty, not to forget the nature, the colors and the sea. But the greatest enchantment greeted them when they were facing spectacular Etna, the majestic volcano! One Wednesday afternoon after returning to Calabria from their brief but intense jaunt in Sicily, after spending the morning on the beach, they stopped in a restaurant near the sea. It was a hot day like many others, but airy. A light wind blew, refreshing and restorative. It really was very pleasant. After a few hours of sun, Francesca's skin had taken on its amber coloring that made her look even more attractive. Her bathing suit generously emphasized her nice curves, and the serenity in her soul shone in her splendid dark eyes. Lorenzo, on the other hand, with his attractive Hawaiian-style bathing suit, with thigh-length pants and showy flowers on bright colors, entertained whoever saw him, not only because of those funny pants, but also because his face and body were as red as a lobster. His fair complexion wasn't made for the violent rays of the Calabrian and Sicilian sun. His wife had tried to make him understand that it wasn't good for him, but she knew that it would be very hard to make him change his mind once it was made up. He liked it and thought he was fine, so he wore it proudly. He had spent the morning between sun-bathing and Francesca's slight teasing. Lorenzo, before stretching out on his nice red beach towel had placed a small alarm clock, which should have rung every half hour, near his ear. The alarm made his hand spring out in search of a huge tube of sun screen lotion, which Francesca had hidden in fun. At the restaurant,

Lorenzo acted as a gentleman and pulled out the chair for Francesca to sit down. He hadn't calculated the fact that, although they seemed made of bamboo, the chairs were actually made of wrought iron and very heavy. So, he pulled his back. Once seated, after a few silent curses against the chairs and a few strategic movements to stretch his poor back, they ordered lunch from the waiter. They chose a truly sumptuous menu. Following the antipasto, they enjoyed spaghetti with anchovies, oil and grated bread. Francesca turned child-like as she recognized those flavors that reminded her of her grandparents and the wonderful vacations spent with them at the beach. She hadn't been in Calabria for a long time, but those wonderful memories were as alive as the blue sky above her. While Francesca was in the restroom, Lorenzo noticed a couple of about fifty, accompanied by a girl who was staring at him. She was surely no more than twenty and Lorenzo looked on perplexed as she, still wearing that infantile expression, began first to wink at him and then to pass the tip of her tongue over her lower lip. In that moment, Francesca returned from the restroom. They stood up and left. Lorenzo turned for a moment as they exited the restaurant and saw that that the girl who first had continued to stare at him was now smiling. He quickly turned back around, feeling a strange excitement mixed with embarrassment. Time passed quickly until, the next-to-last day of their vacation, Francesca's aunt and uncle stopped by to visit for a couple of hours. A minor dispute, springing from the totally diverse political ideas of the speakers, broke out into a violent discussion during which Francesca, taking the side of her relative, angered her husband so much that he left, slamming the door behind him as he went to walk alone. Sitting on a bench, he met the glance of the girl he had seen at the restaurant. He recognized her immediately. She was there alone, wearing a miniskirt and pink top that highlighted her legs and small breasts. She sat on the bench in front of him and threw her head back, showing off an enormous pair of purple sunglasses. She smiled when she saw Lorenzo smiling at her. Lorenzo noticed and stood up abruptly and went to an ice cream parlor. He sat down and while he waited for his cup of fruit ice cream he saw the cheeky siren winding through the tables. She sat at a table near Lorenzo's, took off her sunglasses and started staring at him again. Slowly, underhandedly, she slid her hand until she reached the inside of her thigh. Lorenzo was petrified; he would never have imagined finding himself in such a situation. In short, with complete insolence, the girl told him she would be expecting him in her room that night. She walked up to him and wrote the name of her hotel and room number on a napkin, then slipped it into his hand. The man remained completely blocked, without saying a word or seeming to have any reaction at all. Seeing his inaction, she leaned over him and kissed him on the cheek, while at the same time brushing her hand against his thigh; she continued upward until a satisfied smile was imprinted on her face. The Jezebel man-eater quickly took off and left. He sat there stock-still for several minutes, took another napkin and instinctively cleaned his cheek where she had imprinted that sign of childish lust, then finished his ice cream and left in a daze. That evening, Francesca didn't feel well, unusually nervous and in a bad mood. They quarreled again and Lorenzo, who just a few hours before wouldn't even have thought of meeting the girl, was now standing in the hall of the hotel the name of which was written on the wrinkled paper still at the bottom of his jacket pocket. He couldn't decide whether to stay and go ahead with that absurd adventure or to rush away and clear his head with a nice stroll on the beach. But he stayed there, as though seduced by the song of the sirens. Just standing there remembering that hand, those eyes, that body... He made a miserable attempt at turning toward the entry door and saw the face of the elderly man at the reception desk; he answered the glued-on smile that was always the same and thought of the time that was passing inexorably. The old man asked him timidly, "Can I do something for you, sir?"

"No, I'm expected."

He went toward the elevator; his excitement rose like the winter tide. It seemed to him that everyone was watching him while he waited for that damned box to open up to him like an unread book, or a woman that he had always dreamed about but never had. He looked around, lowering his eyes not from modesty but fear, a bloody fear that instead of blocking him excited him even more, more than more. It was not arriving, it just wouldn't come...no, there it was! He went through the magical doors that disappeared into the wall of the second floor, letting him live his adventure. His blood boiled inside him, in front of the room. There, something irreparable was about to happen. His forehead, beaded with sweat, blocked him; he searched through his pocket to find a tissue, but that tiny piece of paper came out instead, covered with those tiny, childish characters. He walked up to a trash can and threw it away. He then dried off his forehead with the sleeve of his white linen jacket. He was about to knock on the door when he heard voices at the end of the hall, so he waited for a while longer. Silence settled around him once more; with a knot in his throat and his pants bulging, he knocked on the door. His blood began to throb in the vein in his neck; he swallowed saliva in continuation. A few seconds later the door swung open and there in front of him was the object of his desire. Seeing the man, the girl smiled wickedly pleased. She was wearing a black, semitransparent lace negligee through which her small nipples could be seen. She had tied a red sarong around her stomach, a very thin veil that opened slightly over her thighs. A small movement toward the door jamb was enough for the veil to open like a curtain and expose her unripe sex, waiting just for Lorenzo. She emanated a strong scent of violets, her skin was smooth and clear; he tried to enter while searching for the treasure, once more hidden, with a furtive hand. She blocked him and stepped backwards while holding the sarong closed. She was chewing a stick of gum while she placed the palm of her free hand in front of his face. Then she turned her head as though looking at something inside the room. And something was there, something that Lorenzo also saw: her parents. They asked her who the man was at the door and why was she dressed in that manner? Wasn't she ashamed? Didn't she have a bit of modesty? Lorenzo, as pale as a sheet, justified his presence there: he had to return the sunglasses that their distracted daughter had left on the table in the ice cream parlor. The parents of the seductress very courteously invited him in for a glass of wine. He hesitated, but they insisted, dragging him into the room by his arm. Her father was originally Italian and her mother, Irish. They'd been living in Sweden for years, where he worked as a cook, whereas she was employed by an international trucking company. They were there vacationing with their nineteen-year old daughter. Those few minutes were like an eternity for Lorenzo. The couple spoke of their vacation, *of the place's beauty, the little things that he was not the slightest bit interested in. Without being obvious, he looked at their daughter sitting in front of him, next to her parents. At the insistence of her mother, she had put on a very modest white tee-shirt, but she still wore the sarong around her sides. Glimpsing between her legs, which she astutely opened and closed just enough to not arouse her parents' suspicions, drove him crazy as he saw the reason for which he had gone there. The girl was enjoying herself playing with his senses as she sucked her index finger sensuously running it down toward her belly button. Then she stopped with a silent half-smile and started moving her legs again. She was perfidiously diabolic, her parents chatted on without noticing a thing. He though, saw everything. After just a few minutes, having drunk his wine, Lorenzo stood up from his chair, drenched with sweat. He thanked them and left. Right after leaving the room, the girl reached him in front of the elevator doors. He stopped as soon as he saw her arrive. She kissed him on the cheek, leaning on his shoulders, then whispered a sweet "I'll see you tomorrow" in his ear. To finish off her work, she touched his earlobe with her tongue for a moment, smiled and ran back to her room. As he ran from that sort of nightmare, he knew his fate had been decided for him: what shouldn't have happened didn't happen. On one side of the coin he felt let down, but fortunately the idea of escaping from serious danger was gaining ground in his mind, and he knew that he would never again put himself into a similar situation. The evening was slightly cool, despite the heat of the other evenings. He had wandered aimlessly for an hour before returning home, thinking about the stupidity he had been about to commit and trying to get thoughts of that tongue and body that continued to excite him, out of his mind. He had spent his last night in Reggio Calabria alone with his thoughts: his wife was already asleep. He undressed and looked at Francesca's face with its serenely sweet air. He got near her ear and began to kiss it. At first, dozing, she pushed him away with her arm, but then he turned back over her and began to kiss her neck; he clung to her and had his victory over the woman who was still angry with him and pretended to deny him. Their love-making was extremely passionate. He woke up the next morning; upon opening his eyes, he discovered that Francesca had already prepared coffee. The aroma pleasantly filled the room. She came up to him and said a phrase that as soon as it was whispered immediately froze his blood.*

"Good morning, Daddy."

She was in seventh Heaven because she had had the confirmation that she was pregnant and could finally tell him. That was why she had been in such a bad mood the last few days; she had nervously awaited the results of the tests done before leaving on their vacation and which had been late in arriving. She hadn't said anything to Lorenzo even though she had no idea why not. Perhaps she was afraid of his possible reaction or maybe she didn't want to delude him until she was sure. She, who was always strong and decisive, was confused as she never had been before. A mixture of emotions was jumbled up inside her: fragility, fear, immense happiness and insecurity. Lorenzo, after his first moment of shock, called her over to him and placed his hand on her belly. It was then that he realized just who he was and what he wanted. It was as though up to that moment nothing in his life was important when compared to that news. Now he understood. He understood that he was so much in love with Francesca that he wouldn't have wanted to lose her for anything in the world. No, he would never have lost his Francesca or the child that was growing inside her, his purpose in life. Moments like the one he had lived just a few hours earlier with that girl would never again appear in his existence. Only now could he see the sense of what he had been about to do, the stupidity of what could have been his end.

REGINA

Already bright and early the next day the sky was fairly cloudy and the weather was less than promising. The mountain peaks were covered by big, low grey clouds that had been parked there for hours. A light wind blew. Perhaps it would sweep the sky during the day and bring back the sun.

"Good morning, sweetheart." Lorenzo kissed Francesca, still cuddled up in bed, on the forehead.

"Good morning!" she said, stretching. Then, she took his hand, placed it on her face and kissed it. "I'm so tired this morning!"

"Well yes, dear... You know, I think it's going to rain; the sky is full of clouds..."

"Well, that means I'm going to stay in bed a little longer; in fact, let's let the girls sleep... what do you think about coming to keep me company?"

With one hand, she moved the sheets, took Lorenzo's hand, leaning it on her breast and then sliding it toward her belly. He climbed into bed astride her and began kissing her on her neck, on her earlobe and then on the lips. Then he grabbed her legs and slipped inside her. They made love until they fell asleep, exhausted.

"Mommy, wake up. Oh, today she's really tired!"

Carlotta had been pulling the sheet from Francesca's side of the bed and just when she was about to give up, thinking to go drink a glass of water...

"Hmmm… what's happening, Carlotta? What's wrong?"

"Mommy, Ariel and I are awake and we're hungry."

"What time is it?" She looked at her wristwatch.

"Oh, goodness, it's already eleven thirty! Girls, now I'm getting up, if I can. I'm so tired…"

"Yes, Mommy, we slept late, too."

"Have you been awake long, girls?"

"No Mommy, it was just a while ago we went down to the kitchen but you weren't there so we came back up and saw you were still sleeping."

"Well, come up here with us on the big bed. Come here with Mommy and Daddy. Just a little longer and then we'll all go down together!"

"Hey, Daddy, it's really late, wake up!" Ariel whispered in her father's ear.

"Hmmm… I heard, now I'll just stretch a little and…"

Stretching out his arms, Lorenzo suddenly grabbed the girls lying on the bed and hugged them and blew a raspberry on their cheeks. The girls were always happy when he did that trick. After half an hour they all got up and went down into the kitchen, except for Lorenzo, who stayed a few more minutes sitting on the bed. He shook his head thinking about the nightmare that had once again disturbed his sleep. It was becoming more and more intense and this time it seemed that he had read Francesca's name but couldn't remember where: maybe in a big field, but he wasn't sure. Everything was like an unfocused memory. Like the flashes that always took him back into a room with very white walls and a window; flashes of images that seemed real but he didn't know where he had seen them. Then, that incessant pain, those screams; he just couldn't understand what was happening. It disturbed him; those nightmares had been going on for too long. He was afraid. He hoped in his heart there was nothing particular even though he feared – it was useless to hide it – that he had some psychological problem or something even more serious.

Leaving the room, Francesca went into the children's room and dressed them. As soon as she was dressed, Carlotta was the first to take off like a missile. She ran down the stairs followed by her mother's reproaches. The little girl reached Lorenzo and hugged his leg, just as he finished preparing a light breakfast.

"What's wrong, little one?" Francesca asked Ariel, seeing her frown, while slipping on the pink tee-shirt with the white bunny.

"Mommy, I'm sad today, and you can see the weather is, too. Everything's dark… and I don't like it one bit!"

Francesca gave her a little hug. Ariel believed that her humor influenced the weather because one day her grandmother, to calm down one of her sudden tear bursts, had told her that if she had continued on like that, the weather would also burst into a sea of tears. Since then Ariel had been convinced that her tears had the power to make it rain and the weather could be serene only when she was happy. If it rained, it was some other little girl's fault, for sure not hers.

"C'mon Ariel; today we're going to go meet our cow!"

"Oh yes, Mommy! I forgot, now I'll go eat breakfast!"

"Okay, go drink your juice and eat just one donut, not too many like usual…"

When breakfast was over, they walked toward the hut that functioned as an ecotourism and was only a couple of kilometers away.

"Take umbrellas, too… it's going to rain soon, you know, Francesca. Maybe it's better to go in the car."

"No, daddy, let's walk!"

"Okay girls, as you wish."

About twenty minutes later they reached the hut where William the "hutsman" was waiting for them. He was wearing the characteristic heavy wool shirt with colored squares that were often worn in the area, heavy jeans, work boots and Alpine hat. He was very tall, with long hair, blue eyes and an enormous moustache. He was also wearing a blue apron with "Trentino doc" written on it and small mountains, edelweiss and gentian embroidered in the center.

"Hello there, welcome! Ciao, beautiful young ladies!" William greeted the family from the doorstep with a very jovial look, tapping Carlotta and Ariel on the nose and offering them candy. The girls unwrapped one and gulped it down immediately; then Ariel asked him, "Hello, sir, where is our cow?" She had a broad smile that made everyone happy and attentive.

"Let's not lose any more time! Come into the barn, follow me!"

They went into the barn next to the work room. It was well-kept, clean and cared-for. All of the cows, except one huge one, that was there alone, were out in the pasture. Her coat was dark brown with white spots here and there. They all thought she was beautiful. She was eating her hay with great gusto.

"May we pet her, sir?"

"Yes, of course you may… she certainly won't eat you! And just call me Elmo, girls. There are no sires here."

He burst out laughing, soon joined by everyone, even though the girls didn't understand what he was trying to say. They used sire in those parts, with the typical Veneto dialectical inflexion, when speaking to the rich and well-to-do people. Such was not Elmo's case.

"Her name is Regina."

"We know, sir, she's our cow; we have the I.D. card that says she's ours!" They pulled a sort of document, with the cow's picture and her data, from their little purses.

"That's right... of course, certainly you know. How silly of me!" Elmo burst out laughing and continued, "Girls, when you are ready, remember that you should also get what we make with her milk, like cheese, tosella, butter and more."

"Can we take her home with us?" Carlotta asked, glowing.

"The products, yes... certainly! The man said, entertained.

"No, Mr. Elmo, the cow!" The girls turned toward him, but then they turned to their parents with a hopeful look.

"No girls, I'm sending her out to the pasture now, because I think she wants to go out.

"But... but we adopted her sir... no, I'm sorry... Elmo," Ariel said, pushing stubbornly.

"Girls, we can't keep her in the house! She's better off here in the mountains with her friends, don't you think?"

"Okay, Daddy, you're right." Carlotta and Ariel looked at each other and exchanged a nod of agreement.

Adopt a cow was a wide-spread initiative in the Lagorai area, where cows coming from several huts were chosen and an I.D. card was assigned to them. Then those adopting them would pay a certain amount and would receive the corresponding amount in typical products. The gimmick had served to make the mountain life known, with its traditions, tastes and splendid places to visit. It had gone on for several years because of its huge success, especially with children. Elmo showed the family how cheese and ricotta were made and then invited them to have a bite to eat at his home. It was two o'clock and they had a big appetite. After lunch was over and they had said good-bye to everyone, they slowly walked away toward home. After they had gone just a few meters, Elmo called them back because they had forgotten the basket with Regina's delights.

It began to pour when they were almost home.

"Man, what weather... let's open our umbrellas or we'll be drenched."

"Okay, Lorenzo, fortunately we're home."

"What do you say, Francesca, if we go to that shelter they recommended? It's near here! We have to stay inside today, anyway, and I think it will be worth it to go there."

"Okay, it's fine with me, since we'll be back tonight and there'll be time to pack our luggage and straighten up the cabin. We're leaving tomorrow and we have to leave it in order."

"Yes, of course!"

They got into the car and were at the shelter in just ten minutes. It was a building they had passed more than once, but for one reason or another they had never had the chance to stop.

"Good day," said the innkeeper as soon as they entered the inn.

"Good day," Lorenzo responded. They sat at the table to the right of the entrance. "What can I bring you?" a young waiter asked them.

"For me, a ginger and for the girls, a lemon tea. And you, Lorenzo?"

"Well, I'll take that characteristic liquor that you have here; I haven't had one in years!"

"Ah, the parampampoli?" said the young man.

"Yes, yes… that's it!" The waiter walked away, and returned shortly with the drinks: the two teas, the ginger and a ceramic cup that resembled a coffee cup. The size was the same, but it had feet.

"Ha, ha, ha… they already drank everything!" Francesca said, laughing while the children echoed her, laughing coarsely.

"Attention, please!"

A wave of heat hit them all. In a small red pan with a long handle, a liquor burned in the middle of beautiful red flames. The waiter stirred the concoction for a moment and then poured it into the cup until it was overflowing.

"Daddy, it's burning! Look at the flaaames!" Ariel said in awe.

"Yes, Daddy, look… everything's burning inside!" Carlotta confirmed.

"Well then, let's all blow on it together! C'mon, blow hard!" Lorenzo blew the fire out with a soft breath, while the girls blew so hard that a little of the liquid spilled onto their father.

"How is it, Lorenzo? Your mouth isn't burnt, is it?"

"No, dear, it's very hot but drinking it with small sips you can taste it. Mamma mia, it's been a long time since I've had it!"

"May I taste it?"

"Certainly, but be careful; it's burning and pretty strong."

"Okay, I'll just drink a small sip…" Francesca pushed the cup away right after tasting the concoction, trying to guess the ingredients.

"It is strong! But sweet, too… it's good! What's in it?"

"Well, if I remember correctly it has coffee, grappa, sugar, honey… but I don't know the exact recipe. Those are more-or-less the main ingredients…"

"Yes, you can definitely taste the grappa, in fact!" When they finished drinking, they waited for someone from the inn to arrive. The waiter, seeing the empty glasses, rushed over.

"Excuse me; is it possible to go down to the cellar?" Lorenzo asked.

"Just a moment; I'll ask... Yes, you can go. Would you like to drink something else?"

"No, thank you, we'll go straight to the cellar."

"Okay, just follow that group of people." The boy indicated a group that was going through a door in a line.

"Thank you. C'mon girls, let's go, too!" They took off, going down four flights of stairs, and found themselves in a cellar composed of five rooms. It was cold but bearable; of course, they had to conserve the food. The walls of the first room were covered with bottles of wine or grappa. All kinds of cured pork products hung from all over the ceiling... Sausages also reigned sovereign in the second room, together with shelves entirely laden with cheese; there were several hundred rounds, including a giant one in the center of the room that surely weighed more than two hundred-twenty pounds. Lots of smoked hams, characteristic delight of the zone, hung from the ceiling in the third room. In all of those rooms the aromas tickled their appetite, making them want to devour everything.

"Look, Daddy; there's so much stuff to eat." The girls looked upward and continued staring at the products while sniffing that pleasant aroma.

"Hey, girls, do you see that salami there on the side walls?"

"Uh huh..."

"Well, if you look closely, you'll see that it goes around the room three times. It's the longest salami in the world!"

"And it must be the best, too!" Ariel said, laughing as she hid behind her father's legs, having noticed a man laughing at her exclamation.

"Yes, Ariel, I believe it is. However, I doubt that they'll let us taste it, you know?" Walking around the rooms, they tasted a few samples, bought a couple of products and then went back up.

After paying, they said good-bye and returned to the cabin. It was evening and they were all exhausted, truly very tired.

"Shall we fix dinner? Are you girls hungry?"

"No, Mommy, we ate so much!"

"I'm not very hungry, either, Francesca. Between lunch, tasting and sampling, I'm as swollen as a balloon."

"Well, since I'm not hungry either, let's prepare the luggage for tomorrow, my dear girls, and tidy up the place, so…" Francesca didn't finish the sentence because she was blocked by their yells. They pointed to the window with their hands. "Look Mommy… outside the window! It's snowing!"

"No, girls, that's not snow. It's hail; big stones, too!"

"Poor car; oh well, the paint is also made for withstanding heavy hailstorms… I sure hope nothing is ruined!"

"And here we are… the usual Lorenzo worrying about the new car. Don't worry, nothing will happen!" Francesca hugged her husband, folding her hands around his waist and kissing him on the cheek.

"Hey, you make it sound easy… Well, girls, even if we ate a lot, what do you think about warm tea with mountain cookies for dinner?"

"Okay, Daddy… yummy!"

"Oh, Lorenzo… they ate too much and so did we!

"But sweetheart, let's spoil ourselves a little before going home. Then… moments like this… you know it, too; once we begin working, there won't be many, no? Everyone together like now…"

"Well, yes, I guess you're right."

"Good; I'll put the water on to boil and clean up the kitchen; meanwhile, you two help Mommy pack the suitcases and clean up the living room and bedrooms." The girls followed their mother and after half an hour, more or less, of cleaning up the house, they all sat around the kitchen table.

"See, Daddy; we finished," said Ariel, smiling.

"Now I'll pour you some excellent berry tea. Be careful; it's hot."

"I'll get the cookies."

Carlotta pulled the box of pastries from the cupboard. The cookies, heart-shaped, were made with local butter and filled in the center with jam and honey; they were obviously produced locally, which is why the girls called them "mountain cookies".

"You know, Francesca, I've half a mind to run for half an hour, since it has stopped hailing."

"Okay, but go slow and cover up a bit."

Lorenzo went up to the room, put on his tracksuit and jogging shoes, took his iPod, said good-bye and went out. He loved cycling and running when he could. It relaxed him. He put in his ear buds, turned up the volume and began his run listening to music. He had a good run; there were no cars out and he enjoyed the nature and serenity, so rare in his daily life. Everything around moved with him, and he felt pleasure in the exercise, in the sweat that slid down his forehead. That sensation revived him; helped him feel alive in body and mind. He went home and slowly opened the door; he was all sweaty and headed in to take a hot shower.

"Are you guys still here?" Lorenzo asked, wearing his robe, since he was just out of the shower.

"Yes, Daddy. We decided to play charades."

"My daughters are so good!" Lorenzo leaned over and kissed Ariel on her head.

"Are you playing, too?"

"Of course I'm playing, Carlotta!"

"It's your turn, Mommy!" Francesca left the room.

"Okay, what word is it, Mommy?" the girls asked, amused. She indicated the number one with a finger and then put her hands together.

"Pray!" Carlotta shouted. Francesca shook her head for no and then repeated the motion.

"Swim!" Carlotta yelled again, and everyone burst out laughing.

"No, Carlotta…where did swim come from!" "Well, Daddy… you know, I thought she was making a swimming gesture," and everyone started laughing together again.

"Well, let's wait until Mommy finishes giving us clues for the word," said Ariel. Francesca put her hands together again; she put them near her right ear, put her head on them and closed her eyes.

"Sleep!" Carlotta shouted, laughing.

"Very good," said Francesca.

"Man, even I knew this one!" said Ariel.

"Yes, good job, Carlotta; you guessed it: the word is sleep and it's also time for us all to go sleep."

Smiling, Francesca let everyone know that it was late and that they had to go to bed.

They quickly tidied up the room and then everyone went up to their bedrooms. Lorenzo stopped by the girls' room with the idea of telling them a story before saying good night, but saw that they were both already asleep, so he joined Francesca, who was busy putting various creams on her face and hands, in the bathroom.

"You know, I'm really happy for the girls."

"Yes, this place is ideal; they've gotten a rosy color. They've always eaten without complaining and I've seen them have a world of fun while playing."

"Yes, I think it's done all of us good to be in contact with nature."

"Now, though, let's go to sleep, Lorenzo; I'm so tired I can hardly talk."

"You're right, sweetheart. Good night."
They kissed each other tenderly on the lips and fell asleep.

THE CURE

"Doctor, I think we've got it!" Erwin said excitedly, an Italian-American researcher of undeniable talent who had worked in the research laboratory for a year now. Working in such an avant-garde place, especially for someone who had just finished his university specialization courses, wasn't easy; in fact, for many it was only a dream. His was considered a talent, a true genius. His course of studies had led him to two-dimensional nuclear nanotechnologies. He had even worked for six months in the experimental sector of the United Nations, on the moon. He was twenty-eight years old and thin, with his hair shaved down to zero; a good-looking man, even though women and fun didn't exist for him. Research was Erwin's only reason for living. He had a big mole, which he colored purple, right in the middle of his left cheek.

"Really…" answered Ester, head of the laboratory. She was so concentrated on watching the two three-dimensional screens positioned in front of her, she had answered her researcher's exclamation almost as a conditioned reflex.

"Let me see… I'm coming now." She stood up and headed toward Erwin's sector.

"Doctor, doctor!" Molly, the department secretary also called her boss.

"Yes, Molly, tell me."

"They want you on channel two."

"Tell me... are there news?" Ester connected and answered the video call, where the face of an elderly man in a white coat waited for her.

"Ester, the results are still the same as they have been for the last ten years. The curves show a state of complete calm during the day, but only up to certain point, almost always at the same time, when it peaks incredibly for several minutes and then returns to a flat line. This repeats itself every seventy-two hours, for about ten minutes.

"Then they flat-line. According to our theories and the obvious data, we believe we can say with certainty that his status is undoubtedly provoked by the trauma. He has removed everything around him so that he can take refuge in a world all his own."

"I wasn't wrong then, we have it! We're on the right road! When he wakes up we'll ask him if your colleague was right with his theory of the refuge that he created, with which I sincerely disagree." Ester said all this very seriously.

"Are you sure, Doctor?" asked Arianna, a researcher from Florence. Near fifty years old, she had a noteworthy experience and because of this, as well as for her simple advice on both professional as well as human problem, had been an important referral point during the years. One of the few people in the world specialized in dimensional cerebral waves and functionalities hidden in the brain. She was a woman usually calm and measured, cute and a little plump. Married for twenty years, her dream of becoming a mother had finally come true after a long time. She had given birth to two splendid, screaming twins. She had slept very little during the night for the last two years, but her happiness overcame that annoying inconvenience. She was one of the researchers that Ester wanted at all costs, exactly so she could bring about that turning point that they now seemed to have found.

"Certainly, I'm sure; this test, thanks to your diagnosis and the technique we have just applied, are confirming that everything leads to just one direction."

"Are you serious?" Arianna exclaimed, excited.

"Yes. C'mon guys, let's get going since we're on the right path! I want to have that remedy ready within the next few weeks. We're on it!"

DEPARTURE

"Lorenzo, wake up, wake up!" Francesca said, shaking him vigorously in the middle of the night.

"What's wrong, sweetheart?" he answered her; agitated, he turned toward her, turning on the nightstand light.

"You were calling the girls' names out loud; you were moving your arms. You sounded desperate. I was afraid so I woke you up." Saying this, tears began running down her face. She was really very frightened.

"Francesca, you woke me up so suddenly that I still remember what I was dreaming. It's the usual nightmare. I can still see the white walls, and they're freezing when I touch them; there's a crucifix in front of me and a big window. Outside there are two people who are staring and pointing at me; I seem to know them, but I can't understand who they are. And I also hear voices..."

"Voices?" Francesca asked.

"Yes, voices. I saw your face for a moment, and then our daughters as they walked away. I tried to stop you, but I couldn't. I especially remember that Carlotta stopped for a few minutes and turned toward me. She continued to call me, she was crying and I was there answering her, but she couldn't hear me... and then...you woke me up! See, I remember everything..."

"When we get back to Padua we're going to a doctor; it's impossible that you keep having this nightmare, and this time you really frightened me. It could be something serious."

"You're right, dear. I'll make an appointment with a doctor, I swear. Next week, I'll call a doctor, even though I think it's only stress from overworking."

"Well, maybe, dear. Anyway, it's best that you go see a doctor."

"Okay, but let's go back to sleep for now."

Francesca cuddled up next to Lorenzo; she kissed and hugged him, holding him tightly and they slept like that until morning.

"Coffee?"

"Yes, please. This morning you got up before me." Lorenzo yawned and scratched his stomach. He was still wearing his pajamas, and one of the girls' slippers, the ones with the stuffed animal. He had found them in the bathroom, and since his feet were cold, he had slipped them on, even if they were tight and small. The tips of his feet were actually the only part that was covered.

"What time is it Francesca?"

"It's ten, my dear. We slept late this morning, no?"

"Yeah, yeah." Lorenzo frowned for a moment, thinking about what had happened the night before. Then he yawned.

Suddenly, Francesca's cell phone rang.

"Yes, hello? Oh, hi Dad good morning!"

"Hi, Francesca. Forgive me if I'm bothering you, but that big client from Japan is coming in this evening, a week early. He called me and expressly asked for you. What's going on? Are you coming back this afternoon?"

"Well, Dad, our three weeks of vacation are over; if I have to, I'll leave around noon and be back this evening without problems. I'll just leave a few hours earlier, don't worry."

"Thanks, little one."

"And for what, Dad? Don't worry; we'll get that client, it's a given."

"I'll wait for you, then, so we can go to the airport together. Forgive me again, if I disturbed you and say hi to my beautiful granddaughters; I can hardly wait to see them... Uh, say hi to Lorenzo, too."

"It shall be done, Dad. The girls are still sleeping, but I'll go wake them up now, and I'll say hi for you. 'Bye, Dad!"

"'Bye, Francesca."

"Lorenzo... you know, it was Dad and..."

"I heard everything. There are no problems going home early. I know how important that client is to you and I think it's time you dust up on your Japanese. It seems to me you haven't spoken it for several months."

Lorenzo laughed, stood up, took his coffee from Francesca's hand and kissed her on the cheek.

She turned all red; the man's small acts still moved her.

"Go upstairs and wake up the girls, so we can eat breakfast and then leave."

"Okay, I'm going."

Francesca left, but not before caressing his face and looking intensely into his eyes for several seconds. Once the girls were awake Francesca said hi to them from their grandfather, whom they also couldn't wait to hug. He certainly would have a nice gift for them. Their grandfather was good, they thought. She made their breakfast without a hitch; they put a last few things in the suitcases and finished cleaning everything up; Lorenzo went to return the keys of the municipal cabin to the manager and paid the rent for those three weeks, informing him that they would surely return the following year. They took leave drinking a glass of wine.

"C'mon, c'mon, let's load up the suitcases; let's go girls!"

"Okay, Daddy."

"Are you already back?"

"Yes, Francesca, everything is done, without a hitch. We have to come back here sooner or later. It was great, right, dear?"

"Yes, perfect; maybe we could stay here for a weekend, just you and I alone. We can leave the girls with their grandparents. What do you say?" Francesca winked at him and smiled.

"Hmm, good idea. Yes, an excellent idea!" Lorenzo drew near to Francesca and kissed her on the cheek, smiling.

"Okay, let's go!"

"So you're driving like you promised, right? You know, I had a glassful with the manager…"

"Certainly; we'll be in the city in a couple of hours, so there's nothing to it. I need a navigator, though, so who can it be? Let's see…hmm… it can't be Daddy… hmm… let's see…"

"Me, me!" the girls shouted out together, jumping with their arms raised so they would be noticed. Lorenzo and Francesca smiled.

"Okay, so I'll sit in back, understood!"

"So then, I'll say Carlotta will be beside me during the first stretch and for the second, Ariel? Is that all right, girls?"

"Yes," Ariel said enthusiastically.

"Well, yes, all right…" Carlotta said, snorting.

They left and sang mountain songs, the theme songs from their favorite cartoons and the tunes the girls loved the best like "Vicky, the anchovy guitar" and "Shelly, the human pistachio" the whole way home. They stopped off at Bassano del Grappa for a quick stop and to change navigator.

"Okay, Ariel, hook up your seatbelt and let's go."

"Okay, Mommy, I'm navigating now." Arriving at the electronic belt of Padua, Francesca inserted automatic drive, which was obligatory when entering the city. The regulation had been in vigor for a couple of years.

"See how well I drove, Lorenzo?"

"Yeah, very well, indeed… Good, this time I won't say anything." Lorenzo smiled as Francesca started to relax.

"I can hardly wait to take a nice bath when we get home."

"Yes, dear. Maybe the only thing I missed these days is a good swim."

"Yes, the pool!" the girls shouted enthusiastically together. Suddenly, Lorenzo noticed something that wasn't right.

"Just look at that truck taking the curve too fast! Is he crazy?!"

A tremendous bang made the windows in the nearby houses shake. Smoke rose up from the road; black, acrid smoke. Many looked out their windows, many were aware of the accident. People who shook their heads, others who put their face in their hands and cried.

"What happened?" a passerby asked one of the police officers that were surrounding the area with yellow tape.

"A very bad accident; it seems that a truck crossed into the opposite lane."

"Is anyone hurt?"

"Look, it looks like a family of four in that rolled up car you see down there. Frankly, I wouldn't be able to tell you the details; I just got here and was given the order to keep people away from here. They're making assessments, but it seems that the truck's drive shaft gave way or else the inserted automatic drive didn't work. It seems that the truck driver is all right. I don't know anything else."

THE DESERTION

"Doctor Ester, we're monitoring the patient, who just a little while ago had a stronger peak than the others, and we intervened with a tranquillizer."

"Good! Good job, guys!"

"We'll continue staying here and if anything new happens, we'll let you know."

"All right, but everything will finally change tomorrow, or at least I hope so. The experimentation with the cure is over and is positive." Ester watched the faces of the guys in her research team, some who answered her with a nod of agreement, others with a thumbs-up.

"Call Carlotta; tomorrow will be a great day."

"Okay", Molly answered, heading toward her office and picking up the phone. "Hello?"

"Yes, hello…" Carlotta answered, agitated at hearing that voice that rarely called to give her good news, but this time she knew that the call was for one reason only.

"Miss Carlotta, you have to come to the Clinic tomorrow…"

"Okay, but are there news?"

"Dr. Ester told me to tell you that tomorrow will be a great day."

"All right, I'll see you tomorrow; I'll be there around five o'clock p.m. if that's all right with you. Or earlier?"

"Whenever you want, miss; we'll be waiting for you: we certainly won't begin without you." Hanging up, a tear ran down her face, which Carlotta dried immediately. She began moving her hands in search of something to get, to do.

"Who was it?" Her grandfather's form was moving with his cane down the hall toward her.

"Ester, Grandpa. She wants us to go to the clinic tomorrow." Carlotta hugged her grandfather and started crying copiously on his shoulder.

"It was about time!" her grandfather responded with a hard but moved tone. Then he looked at his granddaughter and patted her.

"Courage, Carlotta: you don't want them to see you with swollen eyes tomorrow, do you?!"

"You're right, Grandpa." Carlotta smiled.

"Doctor, they brought them in with the helicopter!"

"How many are there?"

"Just two for now. The others are already there, they're waiting for a supervisor to arrive and assess the case."

"Good, do you have a first evaluation of their conditions?"

"Yes, the girl seems to have a fractured arm and leg. The adult, a forty-year old male, has broken ribs and both upper limbs fractured for sure."

"Okay, bring them to the ER for tests, I'll take a look myself, which is best."

"Where are they?" Lorenzo yelled, regaining his senses as soon as they put him on the ER cot.

"Don't worry, sir, you're in the hospital," the nurse next to him answered.

"Oh my God, what happened?! That truck, that damned truck! Please, tell me, my family… how are they…where are they?"

"Sir, let's think about healing you, then we'll tell you about…" Lorenzo, reading the name on her tag, pressed on, "Miriam, your name is Miriam; please, I beg you to tell me how my daughters are, my wife!" His desperate voice also reached the doctor, who came quickly with an annoyed look and gave a syringe with a tranquillizer to the nurse.

"No, doctor, first I want to know, I beg of you! Tell me, my daughters, my wife; how are they, where are they?" He grabbed a hem of the doctor's white jacket in his hand.

"We're doing everything possible, don't worry." The doctor came near and bent over Lorenzo as he was given the injection.
After just a few seconds, Lorenzo closed his eyes and stopped moving and speaking. His hand, now weak, vainly attempted until the end to keep his hold on the jacket, waiting for a desperate answer. The doctor placed it on his chest, and took several steps back toward the corridor with the nurse, looking at him with compassion.

"Doctor, how are the conditions of his other family members?"

"I've been told that two died. A woman, his wife, and unfortunately one of his daughters, the girl sitting on the front seat. They didn't have a chance. It seems, instead, that the one in the backseat with her father survived the impact, even though she's in desperate conditions. She has a serious internal hemorrhage and we don't know if we can save her."
Even though he had closed his eyes and the powerful tranquillizer was taking effect, Lorenzo had heard everything distinctly.

"Nurse, keep the patient under control; I'll be right back."

All right, doctor."
Drawing close to Lorenzo, she noticed that he was still and his eyes were closed, but tears were running down his face.

"Nurse!" the doctor called her from the corridor; she left the room and came up to him.

"What's happening, doctor?"

"I just heard that the other daughter is going to make it."

"Really?" The nurse's face lit up. The woman turned and went back into the room. She put her mouth towards Lorenzo's ear, convinced of giving him good news, and whispered, "Your daughter is alive; she's going to make it."
Unfortunately, he couldn't hear those words. His soul had eclipsed and his heart was torn apart. They had just abandoned his body, buried by pain.

CARLOTTA

"Hello?"

"Good afternoon, this is Carlotta. I'll be there in about an hour, around six."

"All right, I'll let the chief and Doctor Ester know."

Carlotta hung up and stretched for a moment; she rubbed her eyes, swollen from sleep and weariness. She went into her bedroom, opened her Louis XVI-style armoire and looked at some shirts, twisting her nose.

Suddenly, the radio alarm that she had set for fear of falling asleep went off. Placed on the dresser, it showed both the time and the date. It was June first, 2035.

She pulled on a pair of tight, black jeans, a red tee-shirt with a rose drawn over the heart and a pair of brick-colored boots. Carlotta looked a lot like her mother when she was young, both in her attire as well as in her appearance. Like many girls her age she had a couple of three-dimensional tattoos that, with light pressure, moved for a few seconds, The one on her ankle depicted a dolphin jumping in the sea, and the one on her wrist was a small rose.

"Grandpa, are you coming with me?" she yelled from her room facing the hall.

"Carlotta, don't yell." Her grandfather said, annoyed by his granddaughter's yells. He was very old, now; he actually did have some problems with his hearing but, aside from his limping, he was in pretty good shape for his age, all things considered. He had no other ailments; in fact, he still acted as president of his company, although he had delegated it a couple of years before to a manager of trust and his granddaughter Carlotta. She was like her mother: determined, ambitious, professional and had good business acumen. She also worked fourteen hours straight visiting the different departments and following the production and commercial lines. Respected on both a managerial level as well as by her workers and researchers, even though she was still very young, she was proud to carry on the family business. Carlotta hadn't gotten her degree; she had insisted with her Grandpa Raimondo that she would work after her graduation. After the accident she had taken on many responsibilities and one of these, according to her, was to help her grandfather as her mother would have done.

"Now, Carlotta, don't forget, call me when you get there. I'm staying here today, you know, I don't feel very good…"

"What's wrong, Grandpa?"

"Nothing, I just took a little cold and my usual ankle hurts." Her grandfather, a couple of years earlier, while looking for mushrooms in the mountains, had clumsily put a foot on some leaves that hid a piece of a wet branch. He lost his balance and fell heavily to the ground, twisting the right ankle, tearing the ligaments irreparably.

"I'm going then, Grandpa. I'll talk to you later"

"Bye-bye, Carlotta…. Aren't you going to kiss your poor grandpa good bye?" Smiling, Carlotta kissed her grandfather on the cheek, and then headed to the car. She knew very well that besides the pain in his leg and foot, he was very – too much – moved by the idea that her father could be waking up. He suffered staying there in the hospital; that was why Carlotta hadn't insisted on his going with her.

She sighed when she was just a few yards away from the clinic. Every time she went, she got excited and very agitated, even if it wasn't noticeable. She parked the car, got out and headed toward the entrance.

"Good evening, Miss Carlotta," a nurse said to her as they passed in the atrium.

"Good evening, Germana. Do you know where Dr. Benedetti is?"

"Yes, he's waiting for you in his office."

"Okay, thank you and have a good day." Carlotta arrived at the elevator, pushed the button and waited. When the doors opened she saw Augusto, a young orderly, blond, blue eyes and slightly larger than normal ears, sort-of fan-like. Carlotta really liked him. She blushed and got goose bumps every time she saw him.

"Hi Carlotta, how are you?" Augusto said, smiling shyly. He bit his lip and crossed his hands in front, moving his thumbs nervously.

"Uh, fine, fine. Are you leaving?"

"No, no, I'm going to the garden to get your father who has been enjoying the fresh air for an hour now. I'm taking him back to his room because it looks like it's going to start raining soon..."

"Uh... well, I'll wait for you upstairs; bring me my dad." Carlotta blushed.

93

"Okay, certainly," Augusto said, all excited. His heart was already in his throat and he couldn't say anything else.

Arriving on the last floor Carlotta headed to the chief doctor's office. She stopped before entering, took a deep breath and knocked on the door.

"Come in!"

"Good evening, Doctor."

"Good evening, Carlotta," Dr. Benedetti said with a serious expression. He was a luminary in the medical world, and his Sardinian origins were very clear from his accent. He was an attractive man around sixty years old, always wearing a severe expression.

"Doctor, how is this cure proceeding?"

"Miss Carlotta, I would say that finally, after fifteen years, maybe we can bring your father back to you, today."

Carlotta swallowed and her eyes began to shine. A tear slid onto her right cheekbone, but she dried it immediately, turning her head to the side.

"Are you serious, or just teasing me?"

"Miss, I never joke, especially on medical questions," the doctor said, standing up.
Lifting her eyes, Carlotta became serious.

"Doctor, I know... but I just wasn't expecting it. You know, at the beginning we tried so many cures, but none of them had a comforting effect. When you let me know that you wanted to experiment with a new cure still under study, I didn't think it would be ready so soon."

"You're right, and forgive me for answering you so severely." The doctor spoke to her more for personal interest than out of politeness, remembering that the clinic, destined for long-term patients, as well as the avant-garde research laboratory, had been conceived, built and financed by Carlotta's grandfather.

"Let's go!" They headed toward the wards. The long corridor was flanked by a window through which you could see inside the patients' rooms, all well-cared for and comfortable. Arriving at her father's room, Carlotta saw that he wasn't back yet. She went in and sat on the chair, her chair, where she had sat for fifteen years when she came to visit her father. It was about three feet from the bed.

"Why isn't he here yet?" the head doctor wondered, frowning.

"It doesn't matter, I'll wait; it's not a problem doctor."

"All right, Miss, but he should already be here!" Although upset, the doctor nodded and crossed his arms. Carlotta was very anxious, and the thought that they might scold Augusto didn't make her happy, especially on that day that could be so very important.

While she sat with her hands on her legs, which she moved anxiously, she began to look around the room she had visited hundreds of times. White walls, an armoire, a TV stand and a laptop computer. A photograph of Lorenzo with Francesca, Carlotta and Ariel hung in front of the bed, together with a classic wooden clock with hands that marked time with the typical tick-tock. They had recently brought a bottle of water and set it on the nightstand. Carlotta poured herself a glass. Then, she sat and stared at the enormous window that looked out on the garden. She saw the statue of her mother, with her sister standing at her side, life-sized, in white marble. They were facing the clinic, the room where her father lived. They really resembled the people they were to commemorate forever.

They had created a park with numerous pathways that began in different spots along the perimeter. There was also a large fountain formed at the base of a huge rock where "Ariel" was written in gold letters, turned toward the horizon, toward their grandfather's house. He thought that this way, he would always have his granddaughter beside him. There were many types of plants, trees and flowers in the garden. Ample flower beds set near the clinic entrance formed the name Francesca.

"Here we are," said Augusto, smiling as he entered the room with Lorenzo in the wheelchair.

"Hi, Daddy", Carlotta said in a strangled voice as she drew closer to her father's face and put her hand on his shoulder.

"Well, Mr. Lorenzo, one last effort," Augusto said, carrying Lorenzo's body to the bed, helped by another orderly who had come in with them.

"Is there anything else, Doctor?"

"Yes, stay here in the room; you will take turns: there must always be someone here."

"Daddy, can you hear me?" Carlotta called him, placing her hands on the bed.

"Miss, I have to do the injection now; please leave for now; I don't know how long it will take for the reaction."

"All right, Doctor."

Carlotta stood up and moved her chair to the wall in front of her father's bed and started watching him with apprehension.
The doctor took the syringe and inserted it into the IV in Lorenzo's vein, which had almost become a natural part of his body.

"Now, we just have to wait, Miss; don't worry."

"All right, Doctor." Carlotta smiled in agreement at the doctor and then turned toward the orderlies, especially toward Augusto. She was glad that he was there right then. He made her feel safe. Carlotta crossed her legs. She stared at her father.

-We have just received news that our correspondent has arrived at the place of the accident. Our correspondent Julian is on the spot.
Take it away, Julian.

-Yes, thank you, studio. A new tragedy of the streets has torn apart a family in a section of the curves going from Via Galilei to Via della Repubblica. The road has been closed to traffic for several hours. A family from Padua and a German truck driver were involved in a terrible accident. The truck driver remained uninjured, and it appears that immediately after the impact he got out and assisted the car's passengers first. The family was composed of four people: the parents and two daughters... Unfortunately, one of the girls and the mother were killed in the crash. The violent head-on collision gave no chance of survival to the child in the front seat or the mother, who was driving the car. We apologize, but information is still a bit sketchy. We repeat: a young mother and her daughter have lost their life. It appears that the family was returning home from their vacation in Trentino and that they had started home ahead of time. It appears that the man and the other daughter were seriously injured. Regarding the dynamics, although what happened is still unclear, it appears to be taking shape that the truck was at fault, due to a mechanical breakdown. It appears that it suddenly skidded into the opposite lane after taking a curve. The police are still proceeding with indications from the case. The fire department intervened, pulling the victims from the car, as did the helicopter service which took the injured to the hospital. We remind you that the mother and daughter died on the spot, while the father and other daughter have been transported to the hospital by helicopter. The black boxes from the car and the

truck will tell us exactly what happened in the next few days. For now, the only thing that is certain is that a family was hit by a truly terrible tragedy.

From Julian on the live news web this is all; back to you in the studio.

THE WAIT

"Carlotta, would you like for me to bring you coffee?" Augusto asked. Several hours had now passed and her father, still staring into empty space, gave no signs of change; he was there in the bed, as apathetic and still as always.

"Yes, thank you, Augusto; a weak black coffee, without sugar, please."

"You're not on a diet, are you?"

"No, no…" Carlotta replied with a slight smile.

"Here's your coffee…"

"Thank you, Augusto. That was very nice of you."

"It's nothing. You know, my shift is over now; I have to go pick up my father, whose shift at the factory is up. Otherwise, I'd stay here and keep you company."

"Thank you, but don't worry; we'll see you tomorrow anyway, right?" Carlotta blushed.
"Certainly; I still work here! Ha! Ha! Ha!" He laughed and then continued, "What else can I do except hope that everything goes well?! Try to stay calm, please. My colleague is arriving now; he's very good and nice, you'll see. If there are problems, ring the…"

Carlotta interrupted him, "If there are problems, I'll call you...
but I can only do it if you give me your number. Every time I
come you repeat the same things to me..."
They both laughed and Augusto took a slip of paper and a pen
from his pocket, wrote down his number and gave it to Carlotta.

"There. Now you can call me if you want, but only for
emergencies, please."

Augusto then went right on out; it seemed almost impossible
that he had given her his number. He hadn't done it before
because of embarrassment and shyness. Carlotta was amazed
because he always said he would give her his number, but never
had. But now, they had both tossed it in, like a joke. Now she
had it and was glad.

She had never thought about it seriously before, but maybe her
life would now begin to have room for love, which she had
refused since the day of the accident. The night nurse, Eros, a
fifty-year old man with a reassuring air, came in for the night
shift. His hair was greying and he wore a pair of black plastic
glasses.

The doctor also went by; he entered the room, took the patient's
pulse and listened to his heart. He took out a small flashlight
from his pocket. He turned it on and shone it on Lorenzo's eyes
without receiving a reaction. He pursed his lips and thought for
a few moments.

"You know, Carlotta, this might take longer than we thought; if
you want, you can come back tomorrow morning. It's past
midnight, now."

"Don't worry, Doctor; I'm very patient. I'll wait."

"All right, but I'll have them set up a cot for you next to the bed."

"No, I don't need it, but thank you, Doctor."

"All right, I'll be in the hospital all night; if you need anything, just call me or ask the nurse.

Thank you, Doctor."

Benedetti left.
Carlotta stayed awake almost all night; she napped a little on the chair only around five. The nurse looked on with a paternal air. He wanted to get her a pillow or a cot, but he knew that if he woke the girl up she would have tried to not fall asleep again. He saw that she was determined and he appreciated the love she had for her father. He had worked in that clinic from the first day and he remembered her as a little girl with Mr. Raimondo. He had seen that child come every day. Now, she was sitting there and she had become a woman.
Carlotta woke up at seven a.m. With half-closed eyes, she saw her father in exactly the same position he was in before she fell asleep.

"Would you like some coffee, Miss?"

"No, thank you. I'll stand up and take a quick walk to stretch out a little."

"Well, Miss, I'm still here; don't worry."

"Thank you. If anything changes, please call me. I think I'll go to the cafeteria."

"Certainly."

"Well, I'll be back soon." Carlotta left the room, walked down the corridor and slipped into the elevator. She went for a short walk in the garden. She stopped in front of the statue of her mother and sister. They were truly beautiful. Then she looked down and saw a small daisy that was opening up, slightly taller than her foot. She looked at it for a few seconds; that flower cheered her up for no apparent reason. She turned around and headed toward the cafeteria where she wanted to eat breakfast. She hadn't eaten since noon the day before.

"A cappuccino and two donuts, please."

"Right away, Miss." She took the tray and sat down at a table placed outside the cafeteria. She ate the donut, barely biting it at first and then taking big bites. She had done it that way since she was a child.

"Well, good morning!"
"Oh, good morning!" Ester, already cheerful first thing in the morning, greeted her cheerfully as they passed in the corridor. Besides being the head of the research laboratory, she was also a family friend; she was about sixty years old and was married to one of Lorenzo's best friends, Alessandro. A close friend of Francesca's, she had known that boy who had become her husband thanks to a trip to Trentino with Francesca.

"So, I see you didn't sleep very well last night. Hey, Miss, you know you shouldn't push yourself too much. When Lorenzo wakes up he has to see you in good shape, not worn out."

"Yes, you're right, but I hoped that remedy would work instantly…"

"Of course it works!" Ester said, smiling. "You just need to be patient, you know, because it doesn't act just on the nervous system, but also on the tissues, toning up the muscles so that the patient – in this case your father – can execute at least the most elementary movements after such a long period of inactivity. Otherwise, after a person has been still for such a long time, he would need months to achieve a minimum of muscular independence."

"Yes, I know, but you know how I am."

"Yes, I do, little one. Thank God we can treat many diseases with these new cures. I'm going to your father now; are you coming?"

"Yes, yes… I'm coming; I'll be done in a moment."

"Okay, but take your time, all right?"
Carlotta finished her breakfast, dried her mouth with a napkin, where there were still a few crumbs and then, headed toward the wards together with Ester.

"And how is your grandfather? Is he here, too?"

"No, Ester, he stayed home. It's always hard for him to come here, you know. And then, if my father really does wake up, I don't know if my grandfather could handle the emotion."

"Of course, you're right. First he lost your mother and sister in the accident, his beloved daughter and granddaughter, to then lose your grandmother, too, his great love."
She stood a few moments in silence, then placed her hand on Carlotta's shoulder and spoke in a tone of respect and esteem, "Just think, he has never given up because he had to raise and

educate you, in addition to directing the business… he's a great man! It must have been really hard."

"Uh huh…" Carlotta answered while looking seriously at Ester. Arriving at the floor, they started down the long corridor. Carlotta stopped a moment to look into a room at a little boy with a bandage around his head stretched out on a bed.

"What happened to that boy, Ester? Come here a moment."
Ester was a few yards ahead; she turned and walked back with her classic small, quick steps.

"I didn't see him yesterday, Ester."
As Carlotta spoke, she indicated the little boy with her head.

"Yes Carlotta, I knew that boy would arrive today; he's a desperate case – we are his only hope. He has a disease that we thought had been weakened for several years now."

"What's wrong?"

"A cancer. We're treating him. Just think, we are one of the few clinics in the world able to take care of these rare diseases."
Carlotta's eyes glistened while continuing to stare at the boy, who turned his head and smiled at her, a tender, sweet, smile that only children can give; she smiled back, waving at him with her hand.

"Are you sure?"

"Certainly, Carlotta."

"Okay, I know, but you know…such a small child, it's not fair that he has to suffer…"

"Yes, they're so sweet. But, that's how life is, for good or bad. And you know it, I think!"

"Yeah," said Carlotta, greeting the boy again. He answered her moving his small, weak arm stretched along his body, which he struggled to lift.

"Hi," said the child with a suffocated voice.

"Carlotta, let's go."
The girl hurriedly dried two big tears without letting anyone see her.

"Excuse me, miss..." A child, probably visiting a relative, stood in front of her looking at her.

"Yes?"

"Did you know you look a lot like the statue in the garden?"

"Yes, I know. You know, the tall one is my mother and that shorter one is my little sister." Carlotta leaned down to look into the eyes of that delightfully curious, plump little boy, with his black, curly hair, wearing a dinosaur tee shirt: he was about six years old.

"Oh, your mommy isn't here with you today? Or was she frozen by some kind of rays and turned into a statue?" She smiled at the funny phrase and softly brushed his face.

"You see, my mom is still alive together with my sister; they're here inside my heart. Those statues help me remember that when I'm sad or feel all alone."

"Oh, I see!" Right then, the child's mother called him and he turned, running toward her; reaching her, he hugged her leg. Then, he turned toward Carlotta and said, "Bye, Miss, and say hi to your mommy and sister for me."
Carlotta's spirits were lifted after that conversation. She loved children.

"Here we are," said Ester, looking at Lorenzo still lying motionless on the bed. "Has he moved, by chance, nurse?"

"No, Doctor, he's always stayed just like that, motionless; should I take him out for some fresh air?"

"Leave him here; I see that his muscle tone is coming back. Good! It really is just a question of time. It's better that he comes back when he's in bed. We can't tell what his reaction will be!"

"Do you think he'll be all right? How will he react?" Carlotta asked when she reached the room.

"See, Carlotta, it seems that your father continues to dream about something. Our machines indicate that he gets to a certain point, his brain blocks the impulse; he then plunges, to then return, to give you an idea."

"I see. Let's hope…"

"Don't worry. Are we, or are we not, the best!" Saying this, Ester burst into uproarious laughter, infecting everyone in the room.

"Did I miss something?" Doctor Rossi, assistant manager of the clinic, asked.

"No, no, nothing, nothing… in fact, I have to go; let me know if anything happens. Anyway, everything will be just fine!" Saying this, Ester headed toward her laboratory, still laughing.

"How are you, Miss Carlotta?"

"Fine, thank you, Doctor. And how are you? Is everything all right with your wife and children?"

"Yes, thank you; fortunately, they're all well. Well, good-bye for now; I have to finish my rounds."

"Okay, have a good day, doctor." The doctor left. A world famous heart surgeon from Abruzzi, he had worked there for ten years, teaching and practicing avant-garde methods like the use of water jet scalpels. Many thought he could become a future director. Little more than five feet tall, with blond hair and dark eyes and slightly overweight, he was married to a confectioner from Bologna. His wife had just had a baby girl.

Carlotta sat down and, crossing her legs, picked up a magazine from the table near the TV, a gossip magazine that she usually liked to read for a bit of relaxation.
A couple of hours later she stood up.

"I'm going to go stretch my legs a little," she to the nurse on watch.

"All right, Miss. I'll stay here."
As soon as she left the room, her cell phone rang.

"Hello?"

"Hi, so, how is the situation?"

"You know, Grandpa, it seems that the cure is taking effect. His muscles are toning up some, so Ester says that the waking-up sequence is working."

"Well, c'mon Carlotta, maybe the time is right; let's hope!"

"Yes, Grandpa, if you ask me, Ester knows what she's talking about."

"I know, dear, but however it goes, we won't give up, remember!"

"Grandpa, I miss Daddy's voice so much... however, I'm optimistic." Carlotta's voice broke; her eyes started shining. "Grandpa, I'm going now. I'll let you know if there are news."

"Miss, come quickly!" the nurse said anxiously, running out the door.

"What's wrong?"

"Your father is beginning to move; I've already alerted the doctors!"
Carlotta ran hastily back to the room, her heart in her throat. She was almost trembling. She drew near to the bed while her father was barely moving his hands and feet. He was also moving his head a little. His look was still absent and lost.
With her vice broken by emotion she asked, "Daddy, do you hear me? I'm Carlotta, do you hear me?" She took his left hand and squeezed it between hers to transmit that heat, her love.

THE RETURN

At a certain point, Lorenzo opened his mouth and let out a suffocated moan; a murmur without sense.
The head doctor, his deputy and Ester ran into the room.

"Carlotta, go out for a moment; now, don't worry, we're giving him an injection to stimulate his brain."

There was a great deal of agitation inside the room.
It took an effort for Carlotta to move away from her father. Her eyes were swollen, her face lined with tears.

"My dear Lorenzo, now I'm going to give you a small injection, so you can take your life back into your own hands within a few days. Your daughter needs you." So saying, Ester inserted the needle just under the cervical with a small puncture. Her eyes were shining, too, at the idea of finally being able to give the father to his daughter, who was so dear to her.

"There. Carlotta, you can come close. It will be difficult for him to speak at first, but the cure has been studied for working on the vocal chords, also; so that's also a question of very little time. Call him; make him come back to you."
"Okay, Ester…" Carlotta had been crying copiously for several minutes by now. Tightening her lips, she took a breath and came close to her father. She put the chair next to the bed, drying her tears with her sweater. She began speaking to him, holding her father's hands in her own.

"Daddy, I miss you so much; I need you, your advice, your voice, your smile.

She spoke close to his face, repeating those words in continuation, with a faint smile that held all of her infinite hope and love for her father.

Lorenzo closed his eyes and even stopped moving, keeping Carlotta's hands between his own, Suddenly, he reopened them and began yelling, voicing incomprehensible words and squeezing his daughter's hands tighter and tighter.

Carlotta jumped from the chair and put her face in her hands, frightened. Ester and the head doctor went closer, to keep Lorenzo, who was kicking and punching, still. Fortunately, he was still weak. Ester received a couple of punches in the stomach.
Lorenzo stopped again, and then began yelling and getting restless again. He continued on like this for almost half an hour, alternating episodes every few seconds.

"What's happening, Ester?" Carlotta asked, distraught, almost screaming the words.

"He's coming back to you, Carlotta. Come on, Lorenzo, come back!"
Suddenly, Lorenzo stopped, but this time he stayed still for ten endless minutes.
They were all there, observing him, ready to react at new unexpected gestures, new spasms, or other crises.
Carlotta went near him, her face near his.
However, she immediately backed away, because he immediately began yelling again, and this time the names

Francesca, Ariel, Carlotta were clearly understood. Then, he burst into tears.

"He's returning, he's returning…" Ester said, hugging Carlotta and crying with her.

Lorenzo stopped again; however, he continued to cry streams of tears. Carlotta, letting go of Ester's maternal arm, returned near her father. At that moment, her grandfather also arrived. He was standing with his hand leaning on the door jamb, and his old heart trembled with emotion as he watched that harrowing scene.

"Daddy, I'm Carlotta; do you see me? Can you hear me?"
Lorenzo opened his eyes again and stared at her. Carlotta began to see a glimmer of light in her father's eyes. If happiness could have a shape, be represented as a person, she was sure it would have to be her in that moment. With effort, Lorenzo raised his head toward her. He squinted, his face pallid and gaunt, focusing on that girl who looked so familiar. She stood still, incredulous.

She stared at Lorenzo's hand reaching slowly toward her face…

"Carlotta, Carlotta… is it really you?" he said with a thread of voice, suffocated by tears.

"Yes, it's me, Daddy; I'm your little girl." She took his hand and squeezed it as hard as she could.

"This is a miracle. I thought you died in the accident, too, but you're here instead."

"Instead, I'm here, Daddy; yes, I'm here with you."

Lorenzo's face brightened. He cried because the daughter he thought he'd lost was alive.

Since the day of the accident, unable to bear the immense pain of losing his family, the three loves of his life, he had abandoned his life, finding refuge in a dream, in remembering his last happy days with them.

The walls, the people around him became invisible and silence dominated the room. Even time seemed to stand still watching and their hearts beat immoveable in the echo of their looks. Father and daughter together again. Lorenzo's world was born again and was once more ahead of him, the face of the girl in front of him, who to his tired eyes, full of a new joy, was once again his little girl, his little Carlotta. With an effort, Lorenzo's shaking hand reached his daughter's face and caressed it softly with love.

Index

www.ingramcontent.com/pod-product-compliance
Lightning Source LLC
Chambersburg PA
CBHW020744130626
46554CB00006B/2134